"They tracked you. *Move!*"

"This way." Everly tugged Isaac's jacket and took off. She staggered forward as fast as she could in the blinding conditions, her feet aching from the cold. Isaac matched her step for step. She trusted her feet and her heart knew this place, knew this land.

There! A neon sign warning of a steep descent jutted from a snowdrift.

"Do we go down?"

Her dog gave a low rumbling growl. A man's voice burst through the trees.

"Go!" Isaac shoved her down the incline.

Everly yelped, locking her arms over her chest as she slid. The wind wailed in her ears, and her back smacked into a rock. Pain radiated up her neck, but it couldn't compare to the dread crowding her heart. Blood rushed in her ears as numbing cold seeped in at her ankles and wrists, soaking into her clothing.

"Move!"

The parking lot lay a couple hundred yards on the other side of the ravine, his truck waiting for them.

Right now it felt like a hundred miles...

Kerry Johnson has been conversing with fictional characters and devouring books since her childhood in the Connecticut woods. A longtime member of ACFW, she's a seven-time Genesis Contest finalist and two-time winner. Kerry lives on the sunny, stormy west coast of Florida with her engineer husband, two teenage sons, eight-year-old niece and way too many books. She loves long walks, all creatures great and small, and iced chai tea.

Books by Kerry Johnson

Love Inspired Suspense

Snowstorm Sabotage

Visit the Author Profile page at Harlequin.com.

SNOWSTORM SABOTAGE

KERRY JOHNSON

LOVE INSPIRED SUSPENSE
INSPIRATIONAL ROMANCE

LOVE INSPIRED SUSPENSE
INSPIRATIONAL ROMANCE

ISBN-13: 978-1-335-72268-3

Recycling programs for this product may not exist in your area.

Snowstorm Sabotage

This edition published by arrangement with Harlequin Books S.A.

For questions and comments about the quality of this book, please contact us at CustomerService@Harlequin.com.

Love Inspired
22 Adelaide St. West, 40th Floor
Toronto, Ontario M5H 4E3, Canada
www.Harlequin.com

Printed in U.S.A.

For we walk by faith, not by sight.
—*2 Corinthians* 5:7

For Trevor, Cole and Chase, who make me laugh,
love me well and don't like to see me cry.
(I may cry about this book. It's okay.) I love you.

Acknowledgments

Ali Herring, encourager extraordinaire. I'm grateful to
have such an enthusiastic and caring agent on my side.

Kellie VanHorn, who offered helpful suggestions for
this story and all sorts of other support the past
few months. I'm so glad to count you as a friend.

For my QTs. Your prayers and friendship are precious
jewels of God's grace in my life. #nachosforever

Dina Davis, thank you for your insight and help making
this story shine. I'm thankful to have you on my team.

To Mom, Dad and Mindy, plus all our extended family.
Your prayers and encouragement lifted me
when I fell, over and over. I love you.

Jesus. I will follow wherever You lead.

ONE

She shouldn't have come up the mountain alone.

Everly Raven rattled the chalet's front door handle again. Nothing. The locks on the quaint ski rentals might be ancient, but they held tight, keeping her outside and away from the police laptop she'd been sent to retrieve from the remote, cordoned-off crime scene.

Her heart sank to her hiking boots. Finding her longtime friend and skiing mentor Lars's body inside this chalet yesterday had been one of the worst moments of her life. Even worse than being trapped under an avalanche as a kid. When Lars hadn't returned from his morning milk run on the slopes and hadn't answered her texts, she'd hopped on the lift to check on him.

A sob gathered in her throat. If only she could erase the image of his lifeless body in the chalet, his blank eyes drowning in his pale face, blood saturating the white throw rug. But shaking the memory from her mind proved impossible.

Everly mashed her lips together. With temps hovering near zero and blizzard warnings flashing on her phone, her quick trip up Tipping Point Mountain minus her master key had been a fool's errand. Dirty snow crunched underfoot as she searched. Who had snagged the hidden key from underneath the boot scrubber?

A bitter wind loosened her hair from under her cap, and she tucked it beneath her scarf with stiff fingers. Sorrow and frustration clashed in her chest, making her heart as numb as her hands. In the midst of mourning Lars and worrying about Dad's health, an urgent call had come through from the resort manager, Hugh Markham. *Detective Savage left his laptop in the chalet. The police department is short staffed because of the storm, and he needs you to go up and get it.* Well, she'd tried. Police orders or not, she wasn't getting inside the building today.

Everly searched once more, then aimed a glare at the razor-sharp icicles lining the chalet's eaves. The next opportunity she had, she just might give Hugh and the detective a piece of her mind about sending her up here without an escort.

She stepped away from the front overhang, and a howling gust of wind swept between her and the structure like it wanted to blow her down the mountain. Goose bumps rose under the parka she'd donned before leaving her apartment to do the resort manager's bidding. Hugh had been especially short-tempered and distracted since the gruesome discovery yesterday, and now he'd probably use the fact that she couldn't get inside the chalet as another justification for why Dad shouldn't allow her in a supervisory position at Raven's.

"Alpine! Where are you?" She whistled for her Siberian husky, but the mountain swallowed the high-pitched sound in its wild clutches. The husky was forever in search of unsuspecting critters, and the energetic animal was probably oblivious to the impending storm. Brooding clouds gathered along the horizon, woolen white and swelling with the threat of a massive snow dump.

A blizzard, according to the local meteorologist.

Everly whistled again, then exhaled a frosty cloud of frustration. The police had ruled Lars's death a murder, but nothing about that made sense. Lars was well-liked at the resort, a favorite instructor among ski patrons and employees because of his friendly, dependable personality. She couldn't think of anyone who'd want to do such an awful thing to him. In fact, an alarming feeling had slithered over her yesterday as she answered Detective Savage's pointed questions. If it was murder, as the police suspected, was there a killer still on the loose at Raven's Fun Runs?

The heavy clomp of shoes on packed snow sent a surge of shock up Everly's spine. Definitely not Alpine. But the chairlifts—the whole resort, actually—were closed because of the awful discovery yesterday. Raven's bustling eight-hundred-acre property had emptied within hours, leaving the lodges and two dozen slopes eerily quiet, and now the only sounds were the distant humming of the one lift she'd turned on to ride up Tipping Point, the wind tormenting the trees, and the oncoming footsteps. An unannounced guest at the scene of a murder sent off warning bells louder than the ones they used for controlled avalanches. She slipped around the side of the gray-and-brown building, retreating into a prickly bush.

Two strangers ascended the trail, their steps focused. No police uniforms, nothing marking them as state park officials. The men wore jeans and black jackets with hoods. No hiking boots either. Everly frowned. One of them shouldered a hefty backpack but carried no ski equipment, and they weren't dressed warmly enough to be outside in New England in the dead of winter. They even sported sunglasses despite the overcast afternoon. She shrank against the shingled side of the chalet. Something didn't add up.

"Why do we have to do this now?" one of them groused.

Everly sank deeper into the bushes, careful that the branches laden with snow didn't drop their load and pinpoint her location. The frozen foliage prodded her neck like a knife.

She bit her cheek until the coppery taste of life—and death—burned her tongue. Lars was gone, and now she was huddled alone at the top of a mountain with these strange men?

An intense shiver consumed her body.

At least she hadn't brought Hannah. Her daughter loved riding the lift and had begged to come along, but Everly refused to bring her to the scene of a crime. Plus, the temps were too skin numbing for the adventurous four-and-a-half-year-old, so she'd stayed with Everly's friend and roommate, Becca.

"Ms. Raven? You out here?"

Everly dragged in a measured breath. They knew her name?

He called out again. The way he said her name made her skin crawl.

"He told you she'd be here," the other voice interjected, his thick city accent identifying him as a stranger to the area. "Where'd she go?"

"I don't know. Quit yapping and look around.

We gotta get this over with." A metallic slide and click followed. "Maple Creek. What a ridiculous name for a ski town. I don't see no creek."

Everly's muscles quivered as the men continued in her direction. She leaned sideways until they crossed her line of sight. One of them was built like a beanpole, something black and shiny in his grasp. A gun. Her pulse exploded.

"You gonna let me do it this time?" The shorter man rubbed his hands together, then pointed to the ground. "Wait, are those dog prints? He didn't say nothing about a dog."

"Do you *see* a dog? Find her trail. Our pretty little murderer has to be close."

Murderer? A scalding denial rose in her throat, and she slapped a fist to her mouth. Her elbow bumped a branch, sending clumps of snow downward with a *sploosh*.

"You hear that?" The taller man ducked, then lunged forward. Toward her.

Everly dove through the prickly limbs. The sharp brambles scratched her chin like needle fingers, snagging her scarf so it tightened around her neck like a noose. *No!* She tugged it off and tore around the corner for the back of the chalet.

Where to go? How to get away?

Beneath the deck and hot tub. She ran, slip sliding and breathless, until she reached underneath the wood, seeking the only thing nearby that could take her far and fast down the mountain.

A toboggan.

There! She yanked it out and whipped around as the men appeared, shouting for her to stop. A bullet whizzed past, striking the snow and sending crystal spray up from the frozen ground.

Everly launched headfirst onto the sleek sled, her ribs taking the brunt of the landing. The scream on her tongue cut off as pain seared her middle like a hot pan pressed to her skin.

The sled sank into the powder, settling deep and picking up speed. It sailed down the mountainside. South. This hill led down the backside of Tipping Point Mountain, and no trails or signs marked where she was headed. She leaned her weight, navigating the slim wooden sled to the steeper side. As two loud cracks split across the mountainside, she hunkered into a small bundle and leaned harder, her stifled shriek countering the gunshots.

The constant whoosh of polished wood on snow competed with her roaring breath and the men's angry shouts. No goggles meant the snow churned in her face, stinging her eyes, as she left chalet seven behind.

Her mind sped faster than the sled. Why were they blaming *her* for the murder? She'd answered Detective Savage's questions, submitted a DNA test, then he'd let her go. Everyone at the resort knew she and Lars were like family. They worked side by side, taught ski lessons together, led hikes in warmer months, organized events in the winter season. If Everly was her dad's right-hand woman, Lars had been his left-hand man.

Surely the police knew she hadn't killed him. Surely Dad knew.

One of her boots loosened, bumped the hard-packed snow, then ripped off of her foot and bounced away. She screeched, angling to see it land a dozen yards away. Shoeless in winter meant frostbite, but there was no going back for it now.

Another bullet zinged past, hitting a nearby birch trunk with a thump. Fear squeezed her heart like a giant fist. With recent heavy snow dumps and gusty winds, the thunderous noise could easily start an avalanche. This was backcountry, untouched by ski and boot. The bottomless, unsteady snowbanks were as moody and changeable as Hugh Markham.

God, help me get away. Please, help me make it home safe to Hannah.

Her muttered prayer tore apart in the wind whistling past the toboggan. Was God even listening? He hadn't been for her dad's declining health, or with Mom's terminal cancer before that. And she'd never felt more alone than when her ex-husband, Isaac, left after six months of marriage. *No.* It was years of living at the resort, hiking this terrain and racing her friends down these hills that prepared her for this frightening moment, not faith in a God who felt miles away and never seemed to have time to answer her.

Everly blinked away tears from the biting snow and wind. She'd head for the old caretaker's cottage halfway down the mountain and figure out what to do. No other choice at this point. Only a handful of people knew about the tiny structure. And Alpine—where was she?

After skidding into a snowbank, Everly hefted the toboggan behind a rotting tree trunk and staggered through the woods. Glowering clouds loomed over the isolated terrain, sending gusts of freezing air into her path. She stumbled downhill, her sock icing over, toes numb. *Hurry.*

The cabin was sandwiched between a grouping of boulders and several huge trees standing guard. Shadows smothered the structure like a gray blanket. Everly tugged the old knob forward, then back, to loosen the wood frame. It slid open easily. She glanced behind her, then slipped over the threshold, releasing a pent-up breath.

A man's arm wrapped around her and a

gloved hand covered her mouth, capping off her shocked scream. She was hauled all the way inside, the door slamming behind her.

How did they know she'd come here?

A solid male chest pressed into her back, and she flailed, aiming an elbow at her attacker's rib cage. One thought rose above the chaotic fear spiraling inside her. *Fight.* Her eyes roved the cabin's shadows as she struggled. She couldn't die in here, alone. She had to get out. For her daughter. For her dad.

Hannah's sweet face and big brown eyes filled her mind and emboldened her actions. Everly's screech pulsed through the tiny cabin like a war cry.

But there was no one nearby to help.

Isaac Rhodes grunted as pain spiderwebbed across his ribs, and he barely evaded another of Everly's determined blows. FBI training had prepared him for every possible scenario in the field—except a face-off with the woman who'd once been the love of his life.

"Get off me!"

Everly swung again, only he was ready this time. He'd been on his way to spend the night in the empty cabin when he heard the shouts followed by gunshots. Talk about being in the right place at the wrong time.

"Everly! It's me." Isaac sidestepped, digging out the thin silver flashlight from his pocket. He flicked it on, aiming the golden glow at his chin.

"Isaac?" Everly's wide-eyed gaze skipped from his face to the door and back again. "What— How are you— I didn't think you'd ever come back." Her words came in labored stops and starts.

How many times had he wanted to return? And to apologize and explain why he really left? Except there was no excuse, and right now, there was no time. "Come away from the door." He gestured for her to come closer, but she held still, distrust obvious in her stiff posture. Could he blame her after the way they'd parted?

"I can't believe you're here."

"I heard about Lars."

Everly stared at him with a dazed expression. "I was up there…where it happened. Two men were looking for me—with guns. Why would they want me?" Her shaky words curled into a breathless question.

"Do you have something they want? Evidence?"

"No." She held out both hands. "I told the police everything I knew yesterday. Then Detective Sav—"

"Who sent you up here?"

"Hugh did. He's the resort manager."

Hugh Markham. The man certainly didn't waste time. The former sports agent and US Ski and Snowboard finance committee chair caught the FBI's attention when donation discrepancies came to light recently. Unfortunately, the money trail remained spotless at this point. Not to mention the resort owner in Park City who mysteriously ended up dead while skiing with Hugh. Again, no incriminating evidence tied Hugh to the crime. Yet.

Isaac motioned up the mountain. "That's still a crime scene."

"Hugh said Detective Savage—the officer who questioned me about the murder—told him the chalet was clear." Her chest hitched on an inhale. "And Hugh wouldn't take no for an answer."

I'm hearing that a lot, Isaac almost said aloud. Instead, he flicked his eyes around the shadowed room. Ever since his partner, Dan, pulled Hugh Markham's file last month, an uneasy feeling had set Isaac off-kilter. Partly because Hugh's name seemed to be tied to questionable activities at US Ski and Snowboard, and partly because he now worked at Raven's.

With Everly.

Isaac crossed his arms, fists to biceps. Returning to Raven's Fun Runs meant confronting his past and the mistakes he'd made, but he owed Everly that much. He'd loved her more than anything else in the world, but he let his accident—and his pride—ruin their marriage. Even if she couldn't forgive him for ditching her six months after their wedding, it was his duty to keep her safe now.

And the email he received from the lawyer two months ago sat heavier than a block of ice on his gut. *We discovered the paperwork wasn't signed by the judge...still legally married.*

Her wavering voice interrupted his thoughts. "They called me a murderer."

Now wasn't the time to discuss their legal status as husband and wife. "Did you see Lars after...after his death?"

"Yes." Her face collapsed. "I'm the one who found him."

"That had to be brutal." Also likely set up by Hugh.

"What's brutal is how he died." She gulped another ragged breath. "There was blood everywhere, and I c-couldn't do anything to h-help him. I was too late. And now those men are calling *me* a murderer."

"Anyone who knows you knows that's impossible."

As the agent heading up the investigation for the FBI, Isaac had a growing hunch that framing Everly for Lars's murder was part of Hugh's plan. But why? What was Hugh's angle in this? No way would Everly's dad hand the resort over to Hugh, even with Everly behind bars and out of the picture. Ted Raven loved this resort almost as much as he loved his daughter. Isaac ground his back teeth. *Maybe more.*

Her sniffle turned into a sob as she inched forward and sagged into him. Everly...*crying*?

He roped an arm around her shoulders but held himself apart. Just enough to keep his focus. Because her long-limbed, athletic shape felt familiar—too familiar, as though she belonged in his arms. He cleared his throat and gently set her away.

Everly deserved a whole man, not a broken one.

She wiped her damp cheeks. "I'm sorry. I still can't believe Lars is gone. And now...this."

"You've been through a lot in the last twenty-four hours." A thin thread of crimson crisscrossed her chin, and he withdrew one hand from a glove and ran his thumb gently across the cut. "You're bleeding."

"It's just a scratch."

Scratch or not, the sight of Everly hurt fanned the flame of protectiveness he always felt around her. "What happened? From the beginning."

"I went up to the chalet." She tucked the hair

spilling out of her cap back underneath. It was dark brown and silky as ever. He scowled as the urge to touch its soft texture came and went. "But the hidden spare key was gone, so—"

"Did anyone else know about the spare?"

Her arms fell to her sides. "All the maintenance people do. Hugh does. It's possible one of the officers used it when they first came up to, you know, get inside the chalet."

"Okay. Go on."

"I couldn't find the key, then those men showed up with guns looking for me. I heard them coming, and it gave me a chance to get away."

"How'd you get down the mountain?"

"The toboggan under the back deck."

"Nice. Can't one-up Everly Raven on the slopes." His gaze dropped to her feet. "You lost a boot." He blinked away the blurry vision that plagued him when he was tired or stressed, a remnant of the concussion from his accident.

"It got knocked off on the way here." Her glassy expression cleared, hardening until her eyes pinned him like a stake holding a No Trespassing sign to a fence. "Why did you come back now?"

For her safety he couldn't give much away about the investigation at this point. "I was in the area, gathering information for something I'm working on." He hesitated. "I'm here about Hugh."

"You're writing a story about him?"

"You could say that."

"Oh, *that man*. He's so difficult to work with." She pressed her fingertips to her temples. "I don't understand why Lars and Ingrid recommended hiring Hugh to my dad."

Isaac masked his surprise before responding. "Lars referred Hugh to your dad?"

"I believe so. Ingrid—do you remember her? She's Lars's wife—she had the idea for a new position. *Operations and Construction Manager.* Lars seemed in favor of it too. At least, at first." Her eyes closed for two heartbeats, then reopened, brows pinched. "Lately he seemed so distracted. Upset about the changes Hugh's been making around here. Then I heard Lars and Ingrid arguing last week. I wish I'd been a better friend and asked what was wrong when I had the chance."

"Did you share that with the police yesterday?"

"That Lars hadn't been himself lately?" She nodded. "Yes, I said he'd been stressed about the construction. But not about him and his wife arguing. That seems…too personal."

Seconds ticked off, the harsh reality of Lars's

death settling over her features as he mentally filed away the information she shared. Perhaps Lars wasn't just a victim here.

"None of this is your fault. You had no idea this would happen, Everly."

She shook her head and sniffled, her ski hat slipping sideways.

He edged closer. "As soon as I heard what happened, I had to make sure you were okay." A noise outside drew his attention for several seconds. Just the wind. "Listen, they may track you down the mountain. I need to get you somewhere safe."

"You?" The skepticism in her voice frayed his nerves. "I made it here by myself."

"Of course, you did. You're Everly Raven." He choked down a mouthful of bitterness. She'd always been strong enough on her own. Without him. "Look, there's a lot we need to talk about, but now's not—"

"I thought we had nothing left to say to each other."

His sigh drew from the deep recesses of his chest, where all the old feelings lay hidden and where they had to remain. Everly parroted his words from the email he sent to her along with the divorce paperwork, and he couldn't blame her. He'd hurt her, abandoned her after the accident had separated them.

He shook his head. *No.* No more lies to himself, or her. The accident hadn't separated them. *He* had, by choosing to leave. By realizing that her dad was right—Isaac would never measure up to those flawless Raven standards.

A gust of wind rattled the windowpane as though emphasizing the truth of his thoughts.

"I'm sorry." How inadequate those words were, like building a bridge with balsa wood.

"It's in the past now." She turned, knelt with her back to him and rummaged through an ancient box underneath the back window.

She was right, but he couldn't help the regret that churned in his gut. For the thousandth time he wished he'd never taken that journalist assignment in La Plagne to make a name for himself. Wished he hadn't attempted that double black diamond slope against an arrogant downhill silver medalist before he was warmed up properly. Wished he'd seen that lone tree in time before it knocked him senseless *and* brought him to his senses.

He didn't belong at Raven's, and never would.

A gunshot echoed through the storm. Isaac beat a hasty path to the window beside the door, and Everly followed. They had to move, no matter the weather conditions. The hired killers would follow her trail down the mountain soon. Even in the middle of a blizzard, over treacherous landscape and with snow falling a half foot an hour, their chances dropped lower than the deadly windchill if they stayed here.

She inhaled sharply. "Why're they still shooting?"

"Probably shooting the lock off the chalet door. Did you hear anything else they said?" He moved away from the window, and she trailed him to the small kitchen area.

"One of them said, 'He told you she'd be here,' then he called me a murderer." She blinked across the counter at him. "What if the police think that?"

"They need evidence to back that claim up. I doubt they have any." Last he checked, they didn't. *Please, God, let that still be true.*

A scratching sound followed by an animal whining broke through his weighty prayer. He slapped his palm to his holstered gun, hidden under his coat against his lower back, and threw his other arm out, waving her behind him as he advanced toward the door again. Had they brought in tracking dogs?

"Wait!" She hurtled past and, before he could stop her, threw open the door. A large white dog darted inside, spinning in circles around her, looking way too much like a wolf.

"Where have you been?" She crouched, throwing her arms around the dog's neck and anchoring it still.

The massive breath he'd drawn in released in tiny spurts of relief. "Take it he's yours?"

"*She*. This is Alpine."

He shut the door, then treaded over to the affectionate pair, one of his hands held out. "Hey there, girl. You sure you want to join this circus?" Her canine nails clicked on the wood floor as she wriggled in between them. Alpine sniffed his hand, then nudged his leg with her pointed muzzle, curving her long body sideways to offer him her thickly furred back and tail.

"Now that's a compliment," Everly murmured, as he bent in half to scratch the dog. "She usually takes a while to warm up to people before she demands back scratches."

Isaac finished petting the dog, then stood, and Alpine trotted away, nosing around the new space for interesting smells. All *he* smelled was mothballs and dust in the old cabin.

He addressed Everly with a sober tone. "We need to get you—and Alpine—out of here. Even with the snowfall it won't be hard to spot the toboggan trail down the mountain. And they could've followed your dog." No way was Everly staying near those men. "My truck is parked in the remote lot. We head there."

"Okay." Unhappiness creased the corners of

her eyes and mouth, but at least she agreed to his plan. "There are extra clothes stashed here for emergencies. Let me see if there are any boots."

Isaac remained on the threshold, ears tuning to every sound on the other side of the door. He withdrew his cell. Still no reception. He shoved it back in his pocket, then shot a subtle glance at Everly, confirming one of his chief concerns. Her ski cap was as bright as a neon sign. And she wore designer ski pants and a coat that barely qualified as a parka. Hopefully, it was one of those thin, high-tech fabrics. Still, he wasn't taking any chances. He unzipped his bulky jacket, checking to make sure his bullet-proof vest was still hidden. "I have a new thermal on. You need to wear it."

"I don't *need* anything from you. We—I've— survived just fine without you."

"Suit yourself." The years apart hadn't softened that tough-as-nails, independent streak he'd always admired and respected.

She tilted her head, taking his measure as though she sensed his thoughts. An odd expression—indecision, maybe, or worry—crossed her face. "I can't believe you're actually here."

"There's a lot you wouldn't believe about me now." Like that while he lay in the French hospital in a medically induced coma so the swelling in his brain could subside, his life disintegrating around him, a man named Dan Williams entered it. An FBI agent intent on catching and prosecuting criminals in the professional sports world, Dan had eventually offered Isaac a chance to do something that mattered. Something beyond snagging an interview with the next big athlete or securing the headline of a big-city paper.

At first, Isaac scoffed at the offer. He longed to see Everly and apologize for the argument they'd had before he boarded the plane for France. But Ted Raven, who'd also been at the skiing competition, had visited, and the first words Isaac heard upon waking were his father-in-law muttering how Everly was better off without him. Ted had been furious when Everly booked her own ticket and flew to France. Throughout her short time there, Ted seemed to shadow his daughter in the hospital, giving Isaac and Everly zero alone time, and in private the man mentioned he'd have his lawyer work on getting Isaac's mom's arrest record expunged if Isaac asked Everly for a divorce once he was back home.

Ted Raven's sharp words replayed in his mind like a recorded message. *You're a reckless young man from a broken family, incapable of taking care of my daughter. You have no idea how to be responsible for yourself, let alone a wife. You don't fit in at Raven's, and you aren't welcome there.*

And Isaac realized he was right.

That was when Isaac made the decision. He left Everly and finished an accelerated bachelor's degree in criminal justice while his body healed and the debilitating headaches decreased, followed by one year as a crime analyst at the local police station in Dan's hometown in Maryland. After that, he spent six months training at Quantico before working cases with Dan.

But none of that could be shared with Everly at this point, much as he wanted to clear the air about his whereabouts and activities since leaving Maple Creek. For now, he'd let her think he was still a sports journalist. He hated the dishonesty, but if their situation took a turn for the worse, Dan believed not knowing would keep her safe.

Isaac scowled at the floor. The fact that he came from a broken, dysfunctional family had never sat well with Ted Raven. When they married, her dad had even roasted Isaac when he should have toasted them. Isaac's accident was proof to Raven that his daughter had chosen poorly. *See, that delinquent kid you married never really grew up.*

"Bingo." She held up a pair of brown rubber

shoes with fluffy red socks built into them. Alpine snuffled the shoes, poking hard with her nose and gnawing at them, probably to make sure they were dead, before losing interest.

"Those aren't real shoes. Even your dog agrees."

"They're better than hiking through snow in a wet, frozen sock."

He couldn't argue with that. "Fine. Let's move."

"Isaac, wait." Something vulnerable in her voice grabbed him.

"What?" He hardened the inquiry to counter her soft tone.

"There's something I need to tell you."

An explosion atop Tipping Point rattled the cabin. They rushed outside just as a pillar of fire blazed from the spot Everly vacated less than half an hour ago.

Everly pressed to his side. "The chalet... it's gone!"

TWO

Everly crouched beside the cabin, shoving her foot into the rubber shoe. The summer foot-wear felt strange, leaving her unbalanced and her foot chilled, but at least it would protect her toes from the elements. *For now.*

At the moment they were sheltered from the blizzard's chilly wind by the structure. Once they set off, the falling temperatures and blasts of frigid air would turn deadly.

"You're sure we can't just stay here?"

"No, we have to leave this spot. It's too close. My truck is parked in the lot on the other side of the pit." Isaac aimed a worried eye skyward, where low clouds loaded upon one another like they were targeting the ski resort with snow am-munition. He dropped his gaze to her and ex-tended a wide palm. Just like he'd done in high school as he worked his way into her heart dur-ing track season. She took his hand, rising on unsteady legs.

His strength surprised her. Since his accident and their divorce, Isaac must've pushed himself physically. He'd bulked up, his lean frame now possessing a solid strength. Thick, dark brown hair lay across his forehead, spilling from under his ski cap like when they'd been teenagers, but there was something new in his eyes—a self-assurance that confirmed her ex-husband had become a capable man in the years they'd been apart.

She drew her hand from his and redirected the train of her thoughts.

This was no time to pine over what used to be, especially since he'd made his feelings clear when he returned from France a different man than she'd married, packed his things that weekend, and disappeared from her life. Which he'd likely do again after he finished the assignment he was on.

"Still no reception." He tucked his cell back in his jacket as they made their way out. The flurries increased, turning brown and green branches white and adding more layers to the existing snow beneath their feet.

She'd checked her cell three times since running into the cabin. No service on the backside of the mountain, plus the blizzard would wreak havoc on reception even when they were closer to the resort center. Worry wore paths through her mind. Was Hannah okay? Was she safe with Becca? Why did those men call *her* a murderer?

Everly pulled her arms close on a shiver as continual gusts of coat-whipping wind raged around them. She whistled for Alpine and squinted at their surroundings. "Remember the shortcut to the parking lot? Through the pit?"

He hovered close-by. "I haven't forgotten anything."

Her breath swooped about in her chest like the snowflakes in this blizzard. *Isaac came back.* He hadn't forgotten her. Her traitorous heart pounded out a drumbeat, but she snapped her spine straight to quiet the unwanted noise.

"Neither have I. Especially how fast you left."

How could she forget him, when their daughter looked just like him?

Isaac played with the zipper on his jacket, the gesture so like Hannah that Everly almost gasped. "When we get out of this situation, I hope…"

She tried. Oh, she did. But there was no leaving that bait alone. "You hope what?"

"That you'll give me a chance to explain things to you."

She blinked, her eyes watering from the howling snow circling them. Still, it couldn't blow away his words. After years of silence, Isaac wanted to explain why he left?

Yes, he needed to know about his daughter, but all she could focus on right then was the bitterness of abandonment lodged in her soul. "I'm not sure you deserve that chance." She pushed past him. Her shoe skated across a slick patch, and Isaac's arm shot out, steadying her.

"I should go first. If we hit icy patches, you can fall into me."

She compressed her lips. In more ways than one, she couldn't risk letting him catch her again. "We're in near-whiteout conditions, and I know the way better than you. I'll go first."

He hesitated, then motioned her ahead. Half a century ago, a wide river skirted the base of Tipping Point, until a dam was built on the other side of Maple Creek, drying it up. Her grandfather nicknamed the remaining ravine "the pit." Over the years the land bloomed into a picturesque hiking spot in summer, but it was off-limits during winter months. Posted signs were often ignored, leaving overconfident cross-country skiing patrons with broken limbs and busted skis.

And they were headed directly for it.

They plowed through knee-high drifts, hunched over against the angry wind. Alpine bounded ahead, fully in her element and undaunted by the threatening weather. If only that were the case for her and Isaac. In a blizzard, it was the frigid wind that killed first. They had to make it to his truck and get warmed up, and quickly.

She refused to consider the "or else" in that scenario.

Several minutes passed as they trekked through the blizzard. *South.* They were heading south, but nothing looked right. Her skin tingled from the icy temperatures, and her teeth chattered, jaw tight. Where was the sign? She slowed, panic shadowing every hard-fought, frozen step.

"Everly? What is it?"

"I'm trying…" She was trying to breathe and focus. Trying to figure out if… "I'm not sure which way the pit is. We should be there by now."

"You know this place better than anyone. You can do this."

"But I can't tell which way we're headed. The snow's so thick I can't see Tipping Point Mountain anymore or even figure out what kind of trees are ahead."

He lowered his head, so their faces were inches apart. "Walk by faith, not by sight."

She closed her eyes. *Walk by faith.*

Everly opened them, scrutinizing the ghostly sugar maples and white pines guiding her, giant guards of this land she loved. The land she'd been raised on and was raising Hannah on now. She turned in a 360 to assess their surroundings, Isaac a steady presence nearby. As soon as they were safe, she had to tell him about Hannah, to explain that she'd tried to reach him after his accident to let him know about her pregnancy, but he must've gotten a new cell phone because she couldn't reach him. The familiar hurt enflamed her chest. Most likely, he hadn't wanted to be found.

"What was that?" Isaac stilled, his hand containing her movement, as well.

She tilted her head to listen over the storm, catching a telltale noise in the storm's brief lulls—a constant swishing paired with cracking branches. *Snowshoes*.

Adrenaline discharged into her veins like liquid lightning. Someone was coming.

His grip tightened. "They tracked you. Move!"

"This way." Everly tugged Isaac's jacket and took off. She staggered forward as fast as she could in the blinding conditions, her feet stiff from the cold. Isaac matched her step for stumbling step. She trusted her internal compass, her muscle memory of Raven's.

There! A neon sign warning of a steep descent jutted from a snow drift.

She slid to a halt at a ledge, relief a fleeting

friend. Isaac crouched behind her like he was shielding her from the threat chasing them, and Alpine joined them, her tongue lolling from her muzzle. The ledge overlooked the pit, where a frozen creek snaked through the landscape below, the only remaining tie to the lake that used to fill this void in the earth.

"Do we go down?" The pit would serve as either a shortcut that saved them or nature's mouse trap, ensuring certain death.

Alpine spun to face the woods behind them, a low rumbling growl in her throat raising the hairs on Everly's arms. A man's voice erupted from the trees.

"You're not getting away this time!"

"Go!" Isaac set his hands on her shoulders then shoved her down the incline.

Everly cried out, locking her arms over her chest as she slid. The wind wailed in her ears, and her back smacked into a rock. Pain radiated up her neck, but it couldn't compare to the dread spiraling through every cell in her body. Twigs scraped her coat and frozen flecks of moisture pricked her cheeks as she careened to the ravine floor like a human sled, Alpine leaping and sliding beside her.

Her feet slammed into the petrified trunk of a downed tree. A massive clump of snow slid off, burying her torso, the icy weight blanketing her legs. Blood rushed in her ears as numbing cold seeped in at her ankles and wrists, soaking into her clothing. She wriggled inside the snowy tomb, panic choking off her shout for help. Isaac hit the same tree, then leaped up in one swift motion and pulled her free.

"Move!"

They stumbled forward, Alpine streaking ahead. The ravine floor presented ample open spaces in which they could be spotted from higher ground. Not good. To her left the creek sat frozen, and the parking lot lay a couple of hundred yards on the other side of the ravine, where his truck waited for them.

Right now, it felt like a hundred miles.

"Over there!" He motioned to a pair of fat spruce bracketing a boulder.

She sprinted for the trees. Wedging herself in between the rock and the branches, Everly sank onto folded legs, her breath blasting the needles.

Isaac dropped beside her. "Take off your cap."

"What—why?"

"It's bright pink."

She yanked it off and balled it up. Her ears tingled as the frigid wind howled through the branches and into her exposed skin.

"Where's Alpine?" she gasped.

"I don't know. Lost sight of her when we ran back here. Stay still. I'm going to cut around the rock and ambush him when he gets close. Here he comes."

Everly's pulse throbbed in her temples as one of the men appeared where they'd been barely a minute before. Gray snowshoes glinted across the clearing, and his dark clothes blended with the pit's jagged shadows.

Her eyes widened. It was the tall man from Tipping Point, the one with the gun. He moved in their direction cautiously, flashlight aimed at the ground.

Isaac's hand found hers, giving it two squeezes. Did that mean *move* or *stay still*?

The man's head tilted forward like he was analyzing a map on the frozen earth. Inch by inch, he neared where they were concealed only by branches and snow. A few yards from the spruce, he looked up, staring right at her like she wore a blinking Christmas sweater.

"I know you're back there, Ms. Raven." His calm voice chilled her. "I gotta job to finish, and I wanna get paid, lady."

Anger boiled below the surface of her skin, warming her frozen limbs with the fire of outrage. She was a *person*, not a job. Who hired these men, and had *they* murdered Lars?

Isaac's firm hold anchored her in place.

"I'm not waiting all night." The man pulled something small and dark out of his pocket.

Two clicks followed, and her stomach twisted into painful knots.

Isaac tightened his hand on hers again. Once. Twice. Then he let go, slinking behind the huge rock beside them. His movements were silent and measured, and Everly couldn't catch her breath at how alone and vulnerable she suddenly felt. Where had the second man gone?

If Isaac got shot or hurt because of her, or worse... Everly's mouth quivered. Yes, he had left her when she needed him the most, but he was here now.

"Last chance. Come on out, lady."

A white blur launched from the top of the boulder.

Alpine!

The gunman screeched as sixty-five pounds of Siberian husky landed on his shoulders and sent him stumbling back. Alpine's primitive growl burst through the clearing as the dog ground onto his arm. He jumped up, spinning in circles to shake her off.

"Get off me!" The man's cries morphed into wails of pain. Alpine yelped as the man shoved her off and flung her, but she turned in a flash of white fur and snapping teeth, then leaped again, clamping the same arm between her jaws. A pitiful noise burbled from the man's mouth as he fell to the ground, rolling like he was on fire.

"Get off me! Get it off!"

Another shadow emerged in the clearing. Isaac approached Alpine and the moaning man, crooning low to the riled dog.

"Alpine! Hold." Everly thrust through the branches. "Hold, girl." She scurried closer.

Isaac held a compact black item in his right hand. "Can you get her off him?"

She let out a weak whistle. "Here, girl," she tried, and Alpine released the man. Her canine protector slunk over, trembling from the high-energy attack. "Good girl. It's okay. What a good girl you are." She stroked the husky's thick coat and gaped as her ex-husband took over.

Moonlight showcased the damage Alpine had done. The snow around the stranger was dotted with blackish-red blood, and the man's coat sleeve was torn, exposing red, wounded flesh.

Isaac straddled the man's prone body. "I'll release the dog again if you don't tell me who you're working for."

"I ain't doin' that—ow!"

Isaac pressed his knee in between the thug's shoulder blades. "What was that?"

"Bobby," he slurred. "He goes by Bobby."

Isaac sighed as though he didn't like the man's answer. "You sure about that?" His knee dipped lower.

The man groaned. "I'm sure, man!"

"Where's your partner?" Isaac eased up on the pressure.

"Went ahead. We only had one p-pair of these and I knew how to use 'em."

"What does this Bobby want with Ms. Raven?"

The man let out another moan. "Dunno. Just said to bring her to him and we'd get paid."

"You want her dead or alive?"

"Don't think it matters."

Everly startled at his nonchalant comment, and Isaac tugged a pair of silver circles out of his pocket. Handcuffs? He grasped the man's arms and dragged him toward the spruce tree.

"Hey, where you takin' me? What're you doing? I'm bleeding!"

Isaac ignored the peppering questions and grunts of pain. He positioned the man under the base of the tree, locked the handcuffs around one wrist, then attached them to the lowest branch. He searched the thug's pockets until a small black-and-yellow device fell out.

Isaac picked it off the ground, then strode in her direction.

The man's cries followed him. "Don't leave me! I'm gonna bleed out."

"Not likely." Isaac slipped his gun back under his jacket. In the shadows, his grim gaze met hers. He held the device—some kind of high-tech phone or walkie-talkie—in his hand, before tucking it into his pocket.

"Let's go."

"What about him?" She motioned at the man.

"Someone will be coming for him soon enough."

Isaac avoided meeting her eyes as he brushed past. Everly's legs felt like half-cooked spaghetti. She tossed one more glance at the bloody man, then hurried after Isaac, Alpine glued to her side.

Who was this stranger who'd once been her husband, and why was he carrying a gun and handcuffs?

Isaac drew in a gulp of wintry air to douse the fiery anger that lingered after hearing the perp's threats against Everly. He'd call in the man's location as soon as cell service picked up. It was imperative he keep a clear head for this case, but that was proving harder than expected because of *whom* he was protecting.

Speaking of fire—if only there were a real fire going. With whiteout conditions and dropping temps, the winds had picked up so even his thermals couldn't keep him warm. Ice water flowed through his veins, and he couldn't stop shivering. How was Everly holding up in this? He glanced her way, dread like a lump of coal in his throat. Her shoulders hunched, and her tucked chin quaked nonstop against her chest.

They had to get out of this storm, and fast.

He motioned at Alpine, now trotting ahead in the ravine as though they were on a summer hike and not fighting for their lives. "She's a good guard dog."

"I had no idea she'd d-do something like that." Everly's arm brushed his, but he didn't pull away. Staying close was essential with visibility so poor.

"Yeah, she's definitely protective of you." *Like me*, he didn't say. "I'm glad she knows I'm one of the good guys."

One of the good guys. But was he? He'd made a stupid decision, nearly killing himself on that ski slope in France, and ended up messing up his head in more ways than one. Then he abandoned Everly when life buried him like an avalanche.

Thank You, God, for Dan. The man had pulled Isaac from the pit, set his feet on solid ground. Just like the verse in the Psalms. Dan had saved him, and now he could save Everly. He slid his hand over the gun beneath his coat, tucked in the holster.

Everly's posture stiffened, her discomfort obvious. "You have a gun."

"I do."

"And handcuffs. Are you...a cop now? How did you do that to the guy back there?"

"Not a cop. And I'd say Alpine gets ninety-five percent of the credit."

She remained silent, not pushing the subject of his job. Right now, staying alive was the priority, as well as finding shelter. Because walking in circles meant hypothermia and death.

A pointed rock jabbed his knee as the ground slanted up. They were at the incline. That meant the parking lot was close.

"Hold up." Isaac signaled to stop. His mind was still spinning through the sparse information he'd gained—particularly the name *Bobby*. He'd been sure the perp would say a different name: *Hugh Markham*. As soon as he had reception, he'd notify Dan what he found out. He frowned. He didn't forget names, and that one didn't ring a bell.

He started forward again, and they clambered on their hands and knees up the side of the pit, the driving snow seeping under his gloves and blinding him to all but a two-foot perimeter.

Faint voices carried on the wind. Coming from the parking lot, no doubt. Isaac's jaw clenched. His truck had been discovered, and their transportation was probably shot. Literally. He tapped her shoulder, then shook his head. Close enough.

She huddled beside him and clicked her tongue at Alpine to stay. Even through the white wind, the tense lines of her face were evident. Something seemed different about her...

"Where's your hat?"

Her brows hitched together. "You told me to take it off back there."

"Do you have it?" Her ears would get frostbitten.

"No. I think it got caught in the branches."

Isaac drew his navy one off and fit it over her thick, shoulder-length hair, making sure it covered her ears. He met her wide hazel eyes, then pulled away, closing his to focus on deciphering the men's words.

A car door slammed, and Alpine whined softly.

Everly leaned in, her warm breath on his cheek. "That sounds like Hugh."

The man was involved, but how? Hugh Markham's file sat in the truck's locked glove compartment, fattened up from five years of questionable activity while serving on the US Ski and Snowboard committee and managing a resort in Park City before coming to Raven's.

He wouldn't let the man touch Everly. After what had happened to Isaac's mom—

An explosive shout from the parking lot punctuated Isaac's thoughts. He inched up the incline to better catch the conversation.

"Where is Abbot?"

A different voice answered. "Hasn't radioed in yet… on his way…must've gotten the girl."

"You know that for sure?"

A howling gust swallowed the second man's answer.

"You two messed up on Tipping Point." Hugh again, his words sharper than an icicle. "I told you what to do and you couldn't even make that happen. Find Abbott. Get Everly Raven. Bring her to me."

"Blizzard's blowin', boss."

"I don't care, Eddy! Find her. And find out who this truck belongs to. It's not hers. I don't want to involve the little brat, but I will if it comes to that."

Everly gasped behind him.

"We'll get it done…meeting at checkpoint two."

"Then why're you sitting around blowing smoke? Get going!" A car door slammed. One vehicle drove off, leaving Abbot's partner by himself. Eddy, Hugh called him.

"Yeah yeah, boss. Gimme a break. She's gonna end up a Popsicle by midnight anyway."

Isaac almost smiled. The man had no idea

who they were up against in Everly Raven—or himself, for that matter.

The perp's car engine rumbled to life, and the gritty sound of tires on icy gravel and snow announced the second vehicle's departure. Everly collapsed to the ground, her arms looped around her knees. He backtracked to her side. Her entire body shook—from the cold or from fear? Isaac fought the urge to pull her close—to warm them both up, *not* because he wanted to hold her.

"Why is Hugh doing this?" Her question was a plaintive wail, swallowed up by the wind. Alpine belly-crawled to her, setting her long canine body against Everly like a living blanket.

"That's what I'm aiming to figure out."

"Won't he find out this is your truck and know you're with me?"

"The truck's registered under a different name." That of some fictitious person in New York State.

She was quiet for several seconds, leaning against Alpine's sturdy form. "Hugh's the one behind Lars's death, isn't he?"

Isaac stroked the faithful dog's fur. "We believe so."

"Who is 'we'?" Anxiety flooded her features. "*Who* are you now, Isaac?"

He rotated away so she couldn't see the war waging on his face. Dan told him to keep the investigation under wraps in order to protect Everly. The less she knew, the safer she was.

"I'm working with some friends on a…situation."

"Situation." Doubt underlined her surly tone. "*My* situation?"

He'd never been good at keeping his emotions hidden from her, and *that* hadn't changed between them. He turned to find her arms crossed, her eyes boring into his.

"I'm the same Isaac. With a few more scars and a gun." If only life were that simple. "And right now, I'm asking you to trust me. I'm trying to protect you…and figure some stuff out."

She unhooked her arms and pushed on his chest. "You're not a sports journalist anymore, are you?" She bore down until he was forced to stand to get away from her. To disconnect. Because when she touched him, his concentration melted like spring ice. "Talk about trust. *You* never trusted me, Isaac. Not back then, not now."

"I do trust you. You're probably the most trustworthy person I've ever known. It's just…" He shook his head. "It's safer this way. For you."

"Safer for me? My friend…my coworker," she said, grinding out the words, "was murdered on my family's resort, men with guns are coming after me, my ex-husband appears out of the blue and I have no idea why. *Nothing* feels safe right now." Frantic terror shone in her eyes before she transferred her gaze to Alpine, who paced nearby. "How will I protect Hannah if I don't know what I'm up against?"

He cocked his head. "Who's Hannah?"

THREE

"Everly? Who's Hannah?" Isaac's stare was like a laser beam through her skull.

He might've deserted her once, but he still deserved to know about the child they shared. Her throat was sandpaper when she swallowed. "She's our daughter."

His jaw unhinged. "You were...pregnant when I left?"

Alpine nudged her nose under Everly's arm as though sensing her agitated state and heightened emotions.

"Yes." Why did it feel like the whole world revolved around that simple affirmation? "Her name is Hannah Elizabeth." Her mom's middle name, Elizabeth. The name they'd chosen when they were young and in love, trying to get through college and start a life together.

"A daughter?" He uttered the word like a prayer. "Where is she? Is she safe?"

"She's with my roommate, Becca, at our apartment in Pine Manor."

He dragged a glove across his face. "I'm sorry, Everly. I can't believe you—that we—"

"You didn't know."

How could he? She'd found out she was pregnant a few weeks after he sent the divorce paperwork. Desperate, she'd done everything to get in touch with him. Cell phone, an online search, even contacting one of his estranged relatives. But Isaac changed his cell number, and his uncle didn't know where he was. Eventually she gave up—to protect her heart and Hannah's.

"A daughter." His dark eyes grew misty. Then they widened, and an expression of fury took hold of his features. "Hugh was talking about her when he said *little brat*."

Everly curled her gloved hands together. "I think so."

"What if she'd been up on Tipping Point with you?" Isaac growled.

"But she wasn't." Realization hollowed out her chest. But—what if Becca had needed to work tonight? What if she *had* brought her daughter? Everly pulled her hands apart and ran one over Alpine's sturdy shoulder. Maybe God was watching out for her—and for Hannah too? *Did* He still care? Was He still the God of her youth, who guided her despite her parents' apathy toward Him?

Isaac worried the zipper on his coat again. "We need to get in touch with your roommate. She has to be warned about all this. We've got to keep Hannah safe."

Hearing Isaac say their daughter's name aloud was surreal. She threw off the odd sensation, tugged her cell from her pocket and tried again. Seconds later the short text highlighted in red. "Unable to send." She repeated the effort with the same result. A moan rose in her throat at the same time dread flipped her stomach upside down.

There was no way to call from here. And they were stuck.

"I'm going to check my truck. Keep Alpine back until I make sure it's clear."

He scrambled up the ravine, peeking over the top. Long moments later, he motioned at her. "They're gone. But it looks like they got the tires."

Everly climbed after him, and Alpine darted ahead of her. Concern dogged her steps and each labored breath she inhaled. Her lungs ached at the bitter, frigid air. How would they survive the night outside in a blizzard? Staying in a parked, running vehicle presented a problem—the truck would run out of gas, and the deadly cold would seep in. Only Alpine was accustomed to these brutal temperatures, and the dog couldn't keep both of them warm.

She approached the huge black truck, a dart of unease prickling her neck—or was that hypothermia messing with her nerves?

"I should've parked in the woods." He flicked his cell phone light on, his features gnarled into a scowl. "All four tires are slashed."

Alpine trotted to the edge of the tree line, snuffling the ground. Everly shadowed Isaac as he checked the tires, unable to shake the sense they were being watched. "Do you have a kit to patch them? Or a spare?"

"One kit. One spare." He swept the area with a long glance as though he felt under scrutiny too. "These tires aren't taking us anywhere."

"Gas?"

"Half a tank. Might last two hours. Unless they cut the ignition line."

Panic clawed at her like a wild animal. What if Hannah was in danger, and they were stuck? Forced to stay in the truck for the night, or worse—what if they froze to death?

Movement flashed in her peripheral vision, and Isaac's hand fell to his gun. Alpine burst out of the woods and into the parking lot, then wove back through the trees.

"That dog." Isaac stepped close, guiding

Everly between him and the vehicle, his face turned partially to the woods. "What's she doing now?"

"Probably flushing out animals. She loves being outside when snow's falling." His protective care lifted her from the fog of anxious thoughts smothering her.

"I prefer watching blizzards from *inside* instead of *outside*," Isaac murmured as he positioned his cell and snapped pictures of the deflated tires.

"Me too. Good thing she's equipped to survive outside in this, even though…" She cut the sentence off, and from Isaac's expression, he understood.

We aren't.

Snow fell steadily, blanketing the hood of the truck until the dark color was obscured. The wind lulled for a few moments, and an eerie quiet bloomed as Isaac combed the truck for more damage. Everly gazed into the trees. One of her favorite parts of living on the resort was the disconnect from the busyness that seemed to consume everyone's life. Being outside had once felt like being inside to her—inside God's creation, like a huge, peaceful church of His making. She'd felt safer outside than in, and Isaac had once understood that. Even felt the same.

But between Mom's death, Isaac's accident

and abandonment, and now Dad's illness and Lars's death, Everly couldn't find peace anywhere.

Inside or out.

Isaac opened the passenger door and unlocked the glove compartment, retrieving two manila folders. Was that a file on Hugh? The Isaac she remembered hadn't been interested in guns or handcuffs or crime. Instead, he'd craved stories from the slopes—stories about the best ski competitions, the talented, competitive athletes and the most dangerous runs, even if they took him thousands of miles away when she'd needed him at the resort.

The long-standing bitterness returned, forming a thick wall around her heart. A wall she needed to insulate against the old feelings. "What have you been doing since you left?"

He jerked upright and shoved the folder inside his jacket but didn't meet her eyes. "Full disclosure. Later. I promise."

"You promise?" After promising to love, honor and cherish her, then breaking those vows, how dare he ask her not only to trust him but to believe in this promise he extended now?

Before she could form a response, Isaac ushered her inside the cab and shut the door. He came around to the driver's side, opened the back door to let Alpine into the cab, then climbed inside the front. Pulling out the black radio he'd taken off the tall gunman, Isaac clicked the small knob on the side, and the deafening static made her flinch.

He set the device against his mouth so his words were distorted. "You there?"

The garbled words sounded deeper. Distorted. Isaac's eyes met hers as they waited.

Finally—a crackling noise and an answer. "Abbot, that you? Where you been?"

Isaac clicked the knob. "I have the target. I repeat, I have Ms. Raven."

"Atta boy. Bobby's gonna be real glad to hear that." His partner's voice turned indecipherable. "Meet…ranger station…pick up…drop box… target?"

Isaac breathed heavily into the gadget. "What? Repeat?" He said that two more times before clicking the knob and silencing the shrill static.

"Do you think he believed you?"

His cheeks rounded on an exhaled breath. "I hope so. I'm going to get you more clothes from the truck bed. Stay in the truck and warm up. Then we have to get out of here."

The truck shuddered slightly as he exited and rummaged through the items in the bed. Everly caught her lip between her teeth as she waited. A tender heat warmed her as she recalled Isaac's reaction to learning about Hannah. The back door opened again and Isaac tossed down a colorful, messy pile of coats, boots, and snow gear beside Alpine. A pair of snowshoes snagged her gaze.

Her heart cinched. "You kept them?"

Her wedding present from him stared up at her from the truck's floorboard. The silver and lavender snowshoes—inscribed with a small cursive *ERR* on one side and *IDR* on the other—had been a change of pace from skis, providing a chance to explore areas of the resort she'd never seen before.

Everly licked her cold, cracked lips. She had hopped on a plane to visit Isaac in the French hospital right after the accident, and it had been heartbreaking to see him so incapacitated. Worse was that he'd acted like he didn't want her there. Her dad's critical, hovering presence hadn't helped. She and Isaac had barely spoken, and he'd insisted she fly home with her dad once the competition was over. From that point on, Isaac had missed her calls and texts more and more often. After being discharged from the hospital, he finally emailed her, only it was to announce he was moving on and ask for a divorce.

It had been music to her dad's ears, while she'd cried for a week. She began boxing up his clothes and personal items, and tears drenched each flap of cardboard. Little did she know her emotions were off the charts because of her pregnancy. When Isaac returned to gather his things, she'd tossed the snowshoes in the breezeway and left before he arrived. She hadn't been able to talk to him then, and when the snowshoes disappeared after he did, she assumed he threw them away.

"They've been in storage." He climbed in, avoiding eye contact. "When I knew I was coming back here, I brought them along. In case… I don't know. You changed your mind about them. It doesn't matter now. I figured you'd get rid of them anyway."

A dull ache throbbed behind her eyes. "I would have."

"They were a gift, and…" His gaze found hers then he turned, staring at the snow shoes. "When I was in foster care, I held on to the gifts I'd gotten from my parents through the years. They were material items, sure, but they were the only constant in my life when I was young, the only thing tying *me* to *them*. It was my proof that they'd existed, that we'd existed as a family before…" He shook his head as though dislodging memories from his mind. "Never mind, it's silly."

No, it's not. The words perched on her tongue, but she clamped her lips to keep them back.

She'd believed she was numb to him, to their shared history, but sympathy bloomed in her chest as she remembered all he'd gone through in his difficult childhood. While it didn't excuse his actions, the reminder softened the icy wall shielding her heart.

Still, she couldn't completely let her guard down. Because now she had Hannah to protect.

Everly's gaze fell to the white world outside the truck window. If only things had ended differently. And now, whether she liked it or not, she needed Isaac's help.

He dug around the mess of clothes, drawing out a spare hat for himself. "Where's that pair of boots? They'll be too big, but we can stuff a sock in the tip." He handed her a men's jacket with a hood. Everly tried to grasp it but found her muscles unresponsive. Fear twisted her insides. Had hypothermia set in?

"Here." Isaac leaned close and guided her sluggish arms through the arm holes, struggling to connect the zippers with his thick gloves.

"Better?" His mouth quirked as their breath mingled. He drew the zipper up, slowing near her neck. Their gazes connected as he slid it all the way.

"Yes. Thank you." Her eyes darted to a safer location—the gray dashboard.

"Boots." He handed her a pair of brown hiking boots. A balled-up pair of socks followed. How far would they get tonight on snowshoes? Raven's encompassed two dozen miles of hiking and mountain biking trails. In normal weather, she knew the elevation, as well as the twists and turns of each trail. But in these nighttime white-out conditions, with men after her and her daughter's life at stake, her confidence felt shaky.

When they finished putting on layers of new gear, Isaac tapped his cell. It flashed 7:53. Alpine whined from the back seat, setting her muzzle on the headrest like she was asking what was happening next.

Everly reached back to slide her hand over the dog's head, but her fingers wouldn't cooperate. They felt stiff and numb as she tried to scratch Alpine's thick white fur. Fear wrapped around her rib cage and cinched hard. *Hypothermia.*

While the vehicle's milder interior temperature and protection from the wind helped thaw the prickling numbness in her arms and legs, a vise of dread still gripped her chest. After all, the truck was only a temporary shelter.

"Let's see if the wire is still good," Isaac said, producing his key. "Couldn't see much under the hood."

A tiny spark of hope lit inside her. At least they wouldn't freeze to death—yet. Isaac fit the key in the ignition and turned, only to be greeted with silence. He met her eyes. Then tried again. *Nothing.*

Isaac heaved a long sigh and laid his forehead on the steering wheel. "I'm sorry. They must have cut a line somewhere. I was hoping we could defrost in here."

"Now that you mention it, I do feel a little like a chicken nugget." She grinned, and he startled her by grinning back, eyes crinkled at the edges and miles deep.

"At least it's warmer inside than out. And no wind."

She wiggled her fingers to get the blood moving and distract her from Isaac's close proximity.

Eyeing her hands, Isaac tugged off his gloves. She startled at the familiar sight of his long fingers, squared-off fingertips and strong hands.

"Hannah has your hands." She stuck hers out. "Long fingers, I mean. Mine are short and knobby. Right now, they feel like icicles."

He clasped her frozen digits between his palms and squeezed gently, massaging until she could feel the blood tingling beneath her skin again.

"Is that better?"

"Yes, thanks."

Their eyes met, and in the confines of the

truck's cab it felt like a charged cord connected them. She pulled away, tucking her hands beneath her legs. Her gaze dropped to her lap.

He cleared his throat. "Next step is finding the ranger station Eddy mentioned. We get whatever he left for Abbot before them. It'll be evidence. Are the ranger stations locked?"

"They should be." The small buildings were usually set up with a desk, two chairs, a little fridge stocked with supplies and— "The ranger station has a landline!"

"Okay. We get the evidence first, check if the phones work, then get out of there and find other shelter."

She pressed her mouth into a flat line. Too bad they couldn't stay in the ranger station, but they'd be cornered if they did. What was the expression—sitting ducks? Her mind spun through the nearby chalets. "Falling Waters is a half mile down the service road, but it's being renovated. No roof."

"No go, then. Anything else? Another structure that's enclosed, off the service road?"

Her mind mapped the area. "Roger's cabin isn't too far. Maybe a mile?"

"Roger Dailey?"

She nodded. "He's in town for a couple days, staying with his mom." One of the resort's longtime handymen, Roger had left yesterday to stay with his elderly mother during the blizzard—and to avoid the media frenzy that had descended on Raven's after Lars's murder. "We can go to his place tonight."

A mile hike in this weather could prove deadly, but what choice did they have?

"That'll have to work."

A question nipped the edge of her mind. "Hugh's trying to frame me for Lars's death, isn't he?" She flinched from the force of a sudden shiver and the realization she was in hot water, whether she was guilty or not.

He reached to the back seat, his shoulder brushing hers, and retrieved a small blue-and-red blanket. The dark stubble on his cheek hovered inches from her as he covered her and tucked the blanket gently beneath her shoulders.

"I believe so. Which is why we need to get you out of here and safely to the authorities in Rutland."

"Off the resort? I'm not leaving." Rutland was nearly twenty miles from Maple Creek. "My dad needs me. The place—"

"Is shut down. You said it yourself. You're not staying here, and who knows if Hugh has Maple Creek PD in his back pocket. We'll go somewhere safe tonight, then we'll head to the city. Get your name cleared."

Detective Savage's stern face was seared into

her memory. Still, she wouldn't leave. "I'm not running away, Isaac."

"Everly..." His jaw ticked. "It's not running away. The last place you want to be is near Hugh right now. I'm not sure why he's trying to get to you, but I am certain it's not to help you. More likely, it's to do you harm. I let you down once, and I won't do it again."

She stared at him after his passionate outburst, drawing back at the fire in his eyes and the stark determination in his words. In more ways than one, her ex-husband had changed, and she sensed that fact might add another layer of danger to her life. And Hannah's.

Isaac clamped his mouth shut. Before they'd fallen in love, Everly had been his best friend. While there was no chance of them getting back together, at least he could be the friend he'd always been to her—maybe even a father to their daughter. And right now, that included protecting Everly and Hannah from this manipulative, dangerous man.

He continued, his throat scratchy and dry. "Once we get to the bottom of this and make sure Hugh and those men are in custody, then—"

An enormous *pop-pop-crack* was the last thing he heard before glass shattered inches from his face. Bullets. Everly screamed. He threw himself over the console to cover her, tugging at the door handle on her side while Alpine yelped behind them.

Another shot struck the window, breaking it completely. Glass rained down on them, falling inside and outside the vehicle. Isaac flinched when a shard dug into his neck. Warmth trickled underneath his coat.

Had his voice given away his true identity on the walkie-talkie? No time to consider it. He jimmied the door handle again, and it gave, flying open. They fell outside, Isaac's arm snaking beneath her just before impact on the hard ground. He grunted, then repositioned himself over her, his back facing up. Alpine followed, landing next to them, her legs bicycling the air for a second before tucking beneath her agilely. Everly grabbed for her collar.

"Alpine!" She tugged the dog into their hiding spot. "Stay, girl."

"Lie still." Getting a shot on them in the dark, under the truck, would be nearly impossible.

His focus crystallized. Everly's breath came in tiny bursts against his neck, and he shifted so he wasn't crushing her. He squirmed closer to the sagging tires. Something sharp and hard jabbed his right leg. Glass or metal, no telling.

"Please, God, protect us." Her strained prayer

brought calm to his thundering heart. She'd always done that, her quiet faith pointing him beyond himself to seek God.

"He is. They missed. *Twice*." He could tell that the shots were fired from a far distance, high up, because of the echo off the trees and the direction the bullets hit the window.

"What do we do?"

He tightened his arms around her. "Hold still for now."

"I j-just want to get back to my daughter."

"*Our* daughter," he murmured. "We will." Both of them would make it. They had to.

Moments ticked away, the puffs of their breath slowing. Alpine whined and shuffled her paws in the crushed snow. Frigid air stung his eyes as the winds picked up, which was both bad and good. Hitting a target in these conditions would be difficult.

Two minutes since the last shot. Had the shooter changed locations?

Only one way to find out. Isaac set Everly away from him and reached into the truck. *There.* He heaved the takeout bag from yesterday's dinner into the clearing beyond the truck.

The shooter took the bait. A volley of shots rang out, blowing it apart.

Everly gasped, and Alpine let out a muffled yelp at the sudden noise.

"Shooter stayed in the same position."

"Where are they?"

"Somewhere on the ridge over there." He glanced around. "We need another decoy. Something big enough they'll think it's us in the dark."

"How about this?" She held out one of her snowshoes.

"That'll work." He withdrew the wide metal shoe from her with a grimace. He'd saved them for the last few years, harboring a secret notion that he could return them to her and maybe try to recapture her heart and her trust.

Foolish.

"I need the blanket from the car." It hung halfway out of the passenger side door. He reached up, then yanked it down to his chest.

One snowshoe, one blanket. Would it be enough to distract the shooter and get them out of there alive?

FOUR

Isaac surveyed the finished product. He'd managed to locate a sturdy stick by the front tire, wrapped the blanket around it, then rigged the stick upright in Everly's snowshoe.

"What do you think?"

Her teeth chattered. "What is it?"

"A snow scarecrow. And a distraction." Hopefully enough of one that the shooter wouldn't have time to scope on them.

"How'd you know how to make this?"

"I learned when I was a kid."

Her gaze softened. "In the f-foster home?"

"No, at recess." He shot her a roguish grin. "Though this is the worst one I've ever built." He grasped the edge of the snowshoe. "So, the plan is I'll send this across the clearing, then we take off into the woods, fast as you can. The service road is on the other side of the woods, right?"

"Yes. And the ranger station isn't far from there."

"Good." He pinched the bridge of his nose to

ward off a headache. Sometimes the migraines came on when he was under high stress. Which he was.

"Isaac? You look like you just saw death face-to-face."

He choked back a bitter laugh. Talk about hitting the nail on the head. Everly didn't know about the extent of his head injury from the accident, and it was better that way. Thankfully the headaches had decreased with time. "It'll pass." He rubbed his knuckles on his temple. "Ready?"

"Ready." Her rounded eyes betrayed her confident answer.

He gripped the snowshoe, the metal edges pressing into the skin beneath his gloves. Her life was truly in his hands. He sent a prayer up, into the white abyss swirling around them. *God, please keep Everly safe.* "When you run, zigzag. Not in a straight line."

She nodded. Their eyes met and held, the only thing between them the wild snowflakes.

"One, two, three!"

A forceful shove sent the floppy distraction sliding into the open. The winter scarecrow hobbled when a gust of wind swept through the clearing, sending it sideways with a *thump*.

Isaac wrapped his arms around Everly, and they rolled away from the truck, darted around it and took off into the dark woods. Alpine flew ahead of them like a white streak as more shots rang out.

They bolted into the tree line nearly side by side. Everly's blood pounded in her ears as they crashed into sharp branches and jumped over snow-covered stone walls. The men's boots she wore felt heavy and clunky, shortening her strides.

Trees brushed past in a blur, and her chest heaved with each breath. A car-size boulder rose from the darkness, and she veered around it with a screech, sliding sideways and landing on one knee. She sprang up and shot forward. There, a break in the trees. Alpine's energetic barking echoed off the tree trunks, encouraging her on. Bursting through the woods, she skidded to a stop and bent over, panting, as Alpine circled back and parked on her haunches beside Everly. Before them lay the service road and, a half mile down it, the ranger station. All hidden by the dark and the furious blizzard.

"We made it, girl." She straightened and turned in a circle, then once more. Panic exploded in her middle. She and Alpine were alone.

"Isaac?" Where was he? Had he been shot?

She hadn't heard gunfire, but the wind had deafened her while she ran. "Isaac!"

Everly doubled back to the woods she'd just run through. She flicked on her cell light to find his tracks. Where had he gone after they entered the woods?

Isaac's rumpled form lay a dozen yards away. Everly sprinted over, sliding onto her knees beside him. Snow sprayed into her face. Her heart climbed into her throat at the sight of blood splattered on his sleeve. He lay facedown, as still as Lars yesterday.

"Isaac! Please, God, no! You can't be dead."

She yanked off a glove, then searched his neck for a pulse. *There!* He moaned, turned and struggled to sit, his dark hair askew, eyes glazed. He shook his head. "Still…alive."

Thank You, God. "But you're bleeding. What happened?" She carefully lifted his forearm, and he groaned at the movement. "Did you get shot?"

He motioned behind him with his uninjured arm.

"What?" She squinted at the area he pointed to.

A thin silver wire attached to a half-dozen wood stakes cut across the trees a few yards away. Tiny sharp barbs stuck out along the wire's length. Was that—

"Barbed wire," she said.

His features contorted. "You didn't get…tangled in it?"

"No."

"Glad for that." He puffed up his cheeks, then blew out a pained breath. Alpine snuffled his wounded arm like she wanted to check on him. "You went right, I went left. Guess…the fence was cut at some point. I hit it pretty hard." He winced as he examined the cut. "Doesn't look deep."

"But the wire's old and rusted. We have to find medical supplies. What about in your truck?"

He shook his head. "Can't go back. Does the ranger station have a medical kit?"

"Maybe. They're supposed to have basic supplies." Everly inspected the wound. Not too deep, but blood trickled out. It would need cleaning and bandaging, and now his arm was exposed to the bitter cold.

"Have to keep moving." He gathered his legs beneath him and stood, his large frame wobbly. "Did you hear anything? Car engines, gunshots?"

"I don't think so. Just the wind and Alpine barking."

"You still have…lightning legs."

She fought a smile over the reminder of his

nickname for her from high school track. Isaac had gone to state in the mile, while she excelled in the 400-and 800-yard dashes. She'd always had her parents and friends cheering her on, but Isaac's mom had gone to jail when he was in middle school and his truck driver dad had moved across the country. While his foster family had taken care of him, they'd been busy with their own kids and rarely showed up to the meets, so she'd been his cheering section.

Reality returned, and her smile tightened into a frown. "You'll need a tetanus shot."

"Right now, we need the evidence from that ranger station more."

"You have to get your arm checked out by a doctor ASAP."

"First the drop box. Then a doctor."

"Fine." She clasped his good arm, guiding him down the embankment onto the service road. Typically easygoing, her ex-husband had had occasional moments of stubbornness while they'd been together. Like the trip to La Plagne. His flight fell on the anniversary of her mom's death, plus she'd needed his help at the resort because her dad was traveling to the skiing competition. She'd been aware of Dad's skepticism about her new husband, and—selfish as it might've been—she'd wanted Isaac to stay and prove himself to Dad at Raven's. Instead, he'd insisted that the assignment and resulting article would raise his profile in the sports journalism world.

She blinked into the storm. The trip and the accident had sunk a wedge between them that she had no intention of pulling out. In hindsight, maybe she should've offered to join him in La Plagne instead of thinking only about herself and her family's situation. But really, none of that mattered now.

The wind picked up, snarling their steps as they crossed the road and headed toward the ranger station. Snowflakes prickled her cheeks. Faint tire tracks from Hugh's and his men's cars were nearly covered by the falling snow. Every few feet Isaac turned, looking behind them.

"How much farther?"

Her hood slipped down, and she drew it back over her head. In the distance, a square speck of dark brown stood out among the fir trees. "There it is. Not far."

"Keep Alpine out of the road. I don't want her leaving tracks."

"She's over there." She pointed to their right, where the dog loped along the wood's edge. Alpine stopped and turned, her head cocked as though she knew they were talking about her.

"Keep an eye out. Are any of the maintenance people still on-site? Ski patrols?"

"No. Hugh sent everyone home." A distant rumbling froze her mid-step, at odds with what she'd just said.

Another car, in this weather?

He looped an arm around her waist and dove sideways. They hit the ground hard and tumbled down the embankment, crashing into a massive snowbank. Everly pushed her way out of the frozen tomb, gulping for air.

Beside her, Isaac let out a muffled groan. "Jumping into a pile of snow doesn't hurt like this when you're a kid."

"We're not kids anymore."

He cranked his head left and right. "Where's Alpine? I hope she's out of sight."

Her chest caved in. "Me too." *Please, God, keep Alpine in the trees right now.*

She adjusted her position so she wasn't sprawled on his bad arm. Headlights shone on the road above them, and the crunch of tires on frozen ground and icy concrete grew louder. Fear sent uncontrollable tremors through her. The vehicle rolled past, only a dozen feet away.

"One of the men is out patrolling the service road," he murmured. "Looking for you."

Her phone pinged, and Everly gasped. Service! She yanked it from her pocket.

"It's Becca." A dozen texts from her friend

highlighted the screen, along with a few missed calls gone to voice mail.

"Keep the phone down," Isaac warned. "They're close enough to see the light."

Everly flipped the device over and laid it on her stomach. Her fingers twitched as she waited. After thirty agonizing seconds of silence, he gave her a thumbs-up. Everly slid a fingertip across the screen, found Becca's picture and tapped to call.

Becca answered on the first ring. "Ev! Where are you? Are you okay?"

"We're cold, but okay." She omitted the *on the run* part.

"We? Who's we?"

Isaac snatched the cell. "No details." He mouthed to her, *Tapped Becca's line.*

"Right." Everly set the phone back to her ear. "I meant me and Alpine. How is Hannah?"

"She's okay. She finally fell asleep. She was sad you weren't there to rub her back and read *Goodnight Moon*, but I told her you'd be here tomorrow. Right?"

"I hope so. Tell her I love her, okay? Tell her that Mommy misses her and I'll see her very soon." *Please, God.* Her heart splintered into painful pieces as she thought of her daughter cuddled with her favorite plush unicorn and curled into a C shape under her comforter.

Static crackled as Becca continued. "Why are you still out there? There's a blizzard, Ev. My brother said a cell tower was knocked down near your resort. Can you…"

Becca's words trailed off when Isaac nabbed the phone again and shook his head with a reminder not to mention his presence. She set the phone between them and put it on speaker.

"…why is Hugh saying you're under investigation?"

She met Isaac's narrowed brown eyes. "Where did you hear that?"

"He was on the local news talking to that blond reporter. Said you disappeared and they had no idea where you were, and he was concerned that you had something to do with Lars's murder." Becca let out an incredulous snort. "I didn't catch it all, though. The volume was way down while the news was on because Hannah was still awake. Are you hiding, Everly, for real?"

She ignored the question.

Isaac muted the speakerphone. "Ask if anyone else was with him? On camera, I mean. And make it fast in case your phone is being traced."

Everly repeated the question to her friend after she unmuted.

"Like police officers? A detective was standing there, too, but he didn't say much other than he'd interviewed you." Becca paused. "Oh, hey, your dad called me a couple times, asking where you were and how Hannah was doing. Seemed kind of off again."

Dad. The rumors that she was involved in Lars's death must be wreaking havoc on his health. "What did you tell him?"

"The truth? I said you'd gone to the resort to run an errand for Hugh."

Alpine skidded down the embankment just then, knocking into her and toppling the cell from her hands. Everly gasped as it sank into the snow.

"Alpine!" She dug through the unending sea of white and finally located the phone near Isaac's knee. "Becca? Becca?" Silence met her cries, and tears burned behind her eyes. She closed them and held the device to her heart, ignoring the chunks of snow that snuck inside her gloves as she dug. There'd barely been time to ask about Hannah. Why didn't she warn Becca first about keeping their daughter safe from Hugh?

"We'll keep trying her." Isaac's low, resolute words conveyed his concern for their daughter. "What did she mean, your dad seemed *kind of off again*?"

Everly opened her eyes as her mind shifted gears, from her daughter to her dad. The last couple of months Dad had been distracted—taking calls at odd hours, driving off resort for lunch meetings, not returning for half the afternoon. He'd confirmed he had a female *friend*, but he brushed off the rest of Everly's questions. While she figured there was a new romantic interest, with his health so poor it seemed the wrong time to begin a relationship.

"I think Dad's seeing someone, and that he's hiding it because he feels bad—" Everly swallowed "—because of Mom."

"Your mom passed years ago." Isaac spoke gently. "Seeing someone new isn't that surprising."

Alpine stood and stretched, shaking off the snow stuck to her coat. While Isaac was right, the thought of Dad dating someone else still stung. More than anything, it hurt to think he'd exclude her from meeting the woman who'd caught his interest. "I guess it's not surprising. It's just upsetting because my dad hasn't really dated anyone since Mom died."

"Because he's married to this resort." Isaac's voice held a prickly, bitter undertone.

"What?"

"Forget it. Listen, I've been meaning to ask. Do you have an alibi?"

She frowned at the conversation's abrupt turn. "You mean, where was I when Lars was killed? I was home with Hannah that morning. Then I dropped her off at her preschool at nine and went to work on the resort. Is that good enough?"

He climbed to his feet. "Did you call, text or FaceTime anyone that morning? Did you leave a message verifying where you were, or your plans?"

She rose while repeating word for word what she'd told Detective Savage. "I texted Lars once, about nine thirty that morning. He never responded or read it, and when he didn't show up for his first ski lesson, I knew something was wrong."

"Did Hugh ask about him? Mention Lars that morning at all?"

She combed through yesterday's events in her mind. "No. But that isn't unusual because the two men had very different jobs."

Isaac turned away, but not before she caught the apprehension creasing his face. All signs pointed to Hugh setting her up to look guilty.

"Why is he doing this?" Desperation had a stranglehold on her lungs, so her whispered question was carried away on the wind. Just like the hope she'd been clinging to.

Isaac squinted at the ranger station. He and Everly were hunkered down in the woods across the street, waiting for any signs of the truck's return. Numbness seeped into his fingers and toes, the kind of insidious cold that no material could combat. The blizzard took turns whipping them, the frigid wind obscuring their surroundings with blinding snow. How much longer would it last?

After the call to Becca cut out, they'd waited a few minutes before following the service road to the station. The barbed-wire wound sent bolts of pain up his arm, though in the last minute or so he hadn't felt much. Which was worse. What would frostbite do to a wound like that? Cold air flowed into the gaping hole in the fabric whenever he didn't hold it closed.

Everly pointed. "See the box? That's where they leave tools, files, mail, stuff like that for each other." She turned to him, and it felt like he'd been hit in the chest with a sledgehammer. Minute particles of ice clung to her eyelashes, and her lips were pale and tinged with white. Forget being safe. She needed to get inside the station to warm up, then they'd make their way to Roger's. Fear for her took hold of him like spiked ice cleats on frozen tundra. If not here, somewhere else—and soon. They had to find shelter or they'd die in this storm.

He called Alpine, and the dog trotted over and sat obediently beside Everly.

"Good girl. Stay here." Isaac patted her cocked head, then touched Everly's elbow. "I'll be right back."

He pushed to standing, checked both sides of the road again, then darted toward the box. Reaching for the lid of the square mailbox-like container, he found it stuck. He groaned with frustration, tugging harder. Iced shut. He anchored both hands on the two-inch lip used for opening and closing it. His gloves slipped, and he tried again.

Nothing.

Isaac pounded a fist on the top of the box, earning a tiny nudge of movement. Ice chunks fell. He pulled again with all his strength. The lid popped open, and he stumbled back. Inside, a silver item caught his eye. A key? He scanned the area once more before carefully grasping the item—definitely a key—and placing it in his pocket. A single piece of paper remained.

He slid it out and shoved it into his pocket. They'd read it later.

The hum of a heavy-duty truck engine carried through the trees. This guy was relentless. Isaac slapped the lid shut and spun toward Everly and Alpine, his arm on fire from all the movement.

"Get into the woods!" He sprinted back across the road, away from the ranger station, possible medical supplies and shelter. No time to spare.

She took off, running deeper in the woods, Alpine shadowing her. Isaac sent a prayer heavenward that there'd be no barbed wire on this route. He leaped off the pavement, rolled down the embankment, then shot up to cross into the woods as vehicle lights shone through the snow, falling on his retreating form.

FIVE

Everly grimaced at the blisters forming on her big toes. Each stride, the pain increased. But if those stung, what did Isaac's arm feel like? She shoved away the burden of worry and weaved through the forest after him. Five minutes of running, then ten, gulping icy air that burned her aching lungs. If only she knew the exact direction in which they were headed. In the blizzard, she couldn't make anything out. She couldn't see the landmarks she knew so well and had no idea if they were headed north or south, east or west.

Walk by faith.

Once they'd left the ranger station, Isaac had caught up to her easily, placing himself slightly in front of her—why? To make sure she didn't hit barbed wire too?

They emerged from the trees, overlooking a wide valley. Everly slowed, and the shivering started again. She glanced around. Where was Alpine?

"Why're we stopping?" he called over.

"I think this is Roger's v-valley." A glimmer of light shone across it, a hazy beacon drawing her in the midst of the whiteout. Relief made her dizzy. "That must be his c-cabin. He usually leaves the front p-porch light on." Her teeth chattered out the words.

"Let's go." He pinched the bridge of his nose and shook his head, eyes closed. Was the pale color of his skin from the cold or from pain?

She shook out her hands and arms as they set off down the incline into the valley, then across the snowy field. Deep drifts piled halfway up their legs, slowing their progress. Everly's toes had numbed in the boots. At least it helped with the blisters. Her damp gloves encased her tingling fingers, and weariness tinged with hypothermia pulled at her muscles, making her sluggish and weak.

When they stumbled up the sloping yard, she summoned her last ounce of energy and jogged toward the front porch.

"Hold up. You're sure he's not here?" Isaac peered around, one hand to his side. "Don't want to surprise him."

"His truck's gone. He said he'll b-be at his mom's place until the storm clears."

A large shed that doubled as a garage sat in the cabin's shadow, and the mile-long, winding driveway had disappeared under the storm's wrath. Snow-smothered fir trees dotted the yard, partially masking the cabin's presence at the edge of the valley.

He motioned her ahead. Everly knelt beside the screen door, reaching with uncooperative fingers below the empty cracked flowerpot to retrieve the spare key. She grasped it carefully, then attempted to insert it. The slippery key danced through her uncooperative fingers. When it finally slid in, she opened the door and turned, motioning him in. The cabin's welcoming warmth enveloped her as they crossed the threshold, a sauna compared to the polar vortex outside.

She shoved the key in her pocket and sagged into the wall, gratitude and weariness making her vision blurry. "We made it."

He gave an exhausted nod and looked up. "Thank You, God." He turned his eyes back to her. "He got us here in time."

The Isaac she'd known had been skeptical about her faith and quiet about his own. No longer—yet another aspect of him that'd changed. What a revelation, that his faith was strong now while lately she felt like she was stuck in spiritual sinking sand.

Everly disengaged her hand from her glove and brought two stiff fingers to her lips, letting out a whistle. A distant volley of barking answered.

"Alpine!" she called. "Get in here, girl." An army of tiny flakes blew in along with the white dog, who leaped up the front steps and bounded through the open door. She shook off her thick coat as if she controlled her own mini blizzard.

"Hopefully Roger has something for her to eat." Everly sank to her heels, scratching the dog's pointed ears. Alpine's tongue lolled, her mouth shaped in an exuberant dog grin.

Isaac unlaced his boots and staggered to the couch. "What about me? I'm starving."

"I'm sure he has something for us too." Everly took in the cabin's interior as a flood of relief gushed through her limbs. A recliner sat in the corner, and Isaac sprawled on the worn couch against the far wall, a blanket across its cushions. Between the couch and a TV on the front wall lay a crooked throw rug. Alpine sniffed the rug, then circled and collapsed into a round lump with a contented canine sigh.

Everly pulled off her boots and damp socks, then sank onto the recliner, her mind tracing the familiar, worn pathway back to her daughter. *Their* daughter. Was Hannah able to sleep? *Please, God, keep my girl safe.* If God was listening and He still cared about them, then He must know there was nothing more important to her than her precious daughter.

Isaac dug out his phone, tapping at it for several seconds. "I'm getting reception. I know this is hard, but I don't want you to call Becca—or anyone else, for that matter—tonight. Just in case you're tapped. I have ways…to make sure Hannah is safe."

What did he mean? "I don't like this."

"I don't either. But after what your friend said, it's best to keep your whereabouts quiet until we get some rest and decide where we go next."

She closed her eyes and drew in a measured breath. "Okay." He'd gotten her this far. Kept her safe. Maybe it was time to place a little more trust in Isaac again.

"First let's see what was in the ranger's box."

She rose, followed him to Roger's square table, and they stood side by side. Isaac pulled the items from his coat and clicked his flashlight on, creating a circle of light around them in the darkened room.

She startled. "That's the key to the chalet. See. Number seven."

"The one you found Lars's body in?"

"Yes. What's on the paper?"

He unfolded it, framing it with his hands. A

short message was scrawled across the middle in messy print.

825 Mogul Lane. Finish by midnight 1/18.

Everly's mouth fell open. "But 825 Mogul Lane is Lars and Ingrid's home address. That's tomorrow. And that handwriting...looks familiar." Where had she seen it before?

"They're going to Lars's to finish the job. Destroying evidence would be my guess." He backed away and strode around the cabin. Then he headed for the door.

"Isaac! Your arm? We have to get it cleaned."

His gaze flickered over her head. "First, I need to make a call."

Bitter cold slammed into Isaac as he exited the cabin. After a careful sweep of the yard and snowy fields surrounding it, he pulled up Dan's number and backed into a dark corner of the porch, eyes on their surroundings. One shrill ring—then his partner answered.

"Dan. What do you have?"

"They found evidence implicating Everly."

Shock wrapped his throat like murderous hands. "In the chalet? How? It burned to the ground."

"No. In her office in the main lodge."

Isaac set a fist to his forehead, where the beginnings of a migraine throbbed. "What was it? Who found it?"

"Detective Savage got a tip. He said probable cause justified a search of her office. Isaac, I'm sorry—he found Everly's work shirt tucked in a file cabinet drawer...with blood on it."

Isaac's breath came hard and fast. "Come on! She wouldn't leave it there like that. It could be anyone's."

Dan released a heavy sigh. "Her name is monogrammed on it."

"But anybody could..." Isaac muffled a groan. "They send it to toxicology?"

"Yeah. It'll be days before they know for sure, but..."

"I get it. It doesn't look good." Isaac fought the urge to punch the cabin wall. One of Hugh's men had snuck in and planted evidence. But when? Maybe while she was on her way to retrieve the police laptop. If Hugh would do that, what was stopping him from trying to get into Everly's apartment to plant more?

Hannah. The echo of her name in his mind sent a tidal wave of protectiveness through every cell of his body. His muscles twitched with adrenaline as he paced the porch.

"Listen. This is important. I need a man posted at Everly's apartment. Her friend Becca lives there too." Isaac rattled off the name of the complex. "It's gated, but I don't think that'll stop Hugh or his men. We overheard Hugh and one of his accomplices. He threatened m—Everly's daughter. Please—"

"I'm on it." Dan cleared his throat. "Are you certain Ms. Raven's not involved?"

"Don't." Isaac stopped midstep and glared out at the bleak, bitterly cold night.

"I trust your assessment of the case is based on facts and not emotions, correct?"

"Correct. She isn't capable of killing anyone."

"I defer to your judgment, but between the bloody shirt, Everly disappearing when the police want her for more questioning and the chalet going up in smoke after she was seen taking a lift up there after the resort shut down, things aren't stacking in her favor. So please, tell me something good. What do you have for me?"

"Two men attempted to kidnap Everly on Tipping Point." He relayed the entire story. "They trailed us, and I incapacitated one of them. Well, her dog helped. That man's last name is Abbot. I have his radio. He's handcuffed to a tree beside a large boulder in a hiking area called the Pit. The other man is Eddy, Everly says. No last name." He detailed the incident with the shooter at the parking lot. "My truck's toast. And I recovered additional evidence at a ranger drop box."

"Anything incriminating?"

Isaac shared about the key and the message on the paper and what Everly told him. "The police checked Lars's place, correct?"

"They did a sweep, yes," Dan answered. "My understanding is they didn't recover anything that implicated Hugh."

Of course not. "There's one other thing." Isaac glanced at his injured arm. "I got in a fight with some barbed wire and lost."

"What did I tell you about staying away from barbed wire?"

"Uh, nothing that I can recall."

"Well, I'm telling you now. Stay away from it."

"Thanks for the tip." Isaac chuckled. "When can you get us?" He shot Dan their GPS coordinates.

Silence on the line. A deep breath. "You know we can't blow the cover on this until there's enough evidence to set up a sting."

"Right. But what about a drop somewhere? Or a ride to the center of the resort?"

"Man, that'll draw attention. But I'll do what I can. Regardless of whether I'm your ride, you need to get Ms. Raven back to the main lodge as soon as possible so she can appear for questioning. So, figure out your plan B. I'll obtain a warrant for the deceased's residence in the meantime and see what else I can dig up on Hugh Markham and the other resort employees."

"Yes, sir." Isaac scrunched his eyes shut. They finished the call, then he slipped inside and took off his coat. Everly stood in the kitchen, buttering what smelled like toast. His stomach growled in response.

She looked up, eyes wide like a frightened deer. Then they narrowed to slits. "Follow me."

Always in charge. He exhaled and trailed her down a short hall to a narrow bathroom. The sink, toilet and plain white bathtub took up the entire space, leaving little room for two people.

Everly reached underneath the cabinet, rifling through a plastic tub. Her hip bumped his leg, and he inched through the doorway.

"Get back here." She pulled out a brown container of hydrogen peroxide and motioned for his arm. He carefully rolled up both sleeves of the double layer of shirts over the crusted wound. She leaned close to examine the cut, and the soft waves of her hair fell forward. His fingers twitched with the urge to tuck a loose strand behind her ear.

"How was your phone call?"

He cleared his throat. "Good and bad. I've got a friend who's helping us…on the outside. He's looking into Hugh's past. Running background checks, stuff like that." He settled his hand on hers. An encouraging touch—that was it. "We're not fighting this alone, Everly."

"I'm glad. I mean, that is good news. This is going to hurt." She poured a generous amount of the liquid over the cut, and he bit his cheek at the sizzling pain. The clear peroxide turned rust-colored as it mixed with his blood and dripped into the sink, and she repeated it.

"Sorry." She looked up, and their eyes met and held. "Tell me about the bad, please."

Should he play dumb, leaving her in the dark so she had a chance of resting tonight? No, that wasn't what Everly would want.

He sighed, rolling his head from shoulder to shoulder. "Someone planted incriminating evidence in your office."

Everly set the bottle on the counter and grabbed the white tube of ointment as though he hadn't spoken. She positioned it over the wound and squeezed out a thick blob, then finished with a gauze wrap. He looked away from her shaky movements, hating the internal turmoil she must be fighting. She cleaned up the mess, put the medicine away and slapped the cabinet door shut.

"What did they put in my office?"

"Everly…let's get some rest and we can talk about it—"

"What was it?" Her plaintive words echoed off the bathroom walls.

"A bloody shirt."

She turned on the faucet and washed her hands for so long steam rose from the hot water. "I can't believe they did this. Hugh did this."

"He's a criminal who doesn't play fair."

"He always seemed dishonest and selfish, like he didn't care about anyone or anything but his own plans for the resort. But murdering Lars, and blaming me? This could put me behind bars, right?"

Like my mom.

He'd been twelve when Mom had finally landed a full-time job on the cleaning crew of a hotel in a nearby city. Once she provided a stable income and maintained her apartment rent, no more foster homes for him. But a couple of months in, she'd gotten caught up with a local drug ring that threatened her job if she didn't help. Her small role had snowballed into a lengthy sentence at a women's correction facility.

After that, any hope of reuniting with his mom had been dashed.

Isaac couldn't gather a response in time before she continued.

"Can we at least use the evidence you found at the ranger station against him?"

"I plan to give it to the authorities, yes. But at this point, that's not much to go on. There's no name. The perpetrator in the pit used the name Bobby. We need a solid connection between Hugh and Lars or Hugh and this Bobby, like an argument via email or a disagreement witnessed by others. Physical evidence would be best. And a motive. We still don't know why he's doing all this."

She slipped past him, into the hall. He finished cleaning himself up, washed his hands, then followed her into the kitchen. Alpine still lay curled up on the rug like a cat, muzzle covered by her tail.

"Here." Everly set two pieces of toast before him. Smeared with a generous helping of peanut butter and butter, just the way he liked. He murmured *thank you* and tucked into them. She handed him a water and set her chin on her threaded fingers, watching him with a shuttered, unreadable expression.

Halfway through the second piece, he met her troubled eyes. "Aren't you going to eat?"

"I don't have much of an appetite right now."

"You have to eat something."

She mumbled a sound of reluctant agreement and turned to make herself toast, then carried a sandwich over to Alpine too. When she returned to the kitchen area, the shadows on her face had lightened like clouds parting after a storm.

"Maybe I can help with the motive part."

He swiped at his mouth. Had she been hiding something from him? "How so?"

"Our IT guy was working on the resort server last week, and Hugh wasn't available, so Chris asked if *I* wanted to set the new passwords. I can get into all of Hugh's emails since he came to Raven's." She angled her face toward the ceiling. "Roger's computer is in the loft."

Everly sat cross-legged on the futon in Roger's narrow loft, her contact list of Raven's employees opened on her cell phone. Isaac tapped his fingers on the desk beside her, waiting for the ancient desktop computer to come to life. Shadows danced on the walls as flurries hounded the house. They'd kept all the inside lights off, and the brightness of her cell screen made her squint.

Every twenty seconds or so, Isaac peered out the second-story window at the dark, snow-swept landscape. "Still coming down."

"It's supposed to continue through the night."

"Better for us."

But was it? What if the men stumbled across Roger's cabin and decided to find shelter too? Goose bumps prickled her skin despite the afghan thrown over her lap. Alpine would hear someone approach in this howling banshee of a blizzard, wouldn't she?

"Any idea who else might be on Hugh's personal payroll?" His gaze flickered to her, then returned to the computer.

They'd been over the list twice now, Everly repeating employee names and their positions. "No Bobby or Bob that I know of. And as far as being in cahoots with Hugh, most of the staff just puts up with him. No one seems to like him." She catalogued every memory she could recall. "He has a guy—James, I think—who visits from time to time."

"This James fellow have a last name?"

"I don't remember. He's from Park City, Hugh said. Military look to him. Barely speaks, never smiles."

"Sounds like a bodyguard."

"Yeah, well, Hugh hasn't exactly made lots of friends around here. Even the supply and delivery people who come on property avoid him." She swiped her contact list closed.

"Finally, this thing's turning on."

Roger's computer lit up with an enlarged picture of the scene out the front door—a snowy meadow surrounded by a picturesque wall of fir trees leading up the rise of Raven's Peak. The winter sunset burned the sky orange. It was a quintessential Raven's shot, taken by a paid photographer for an informational brochure she'd designed a few years back.

Everly's eyes misted. "My home. Hannah's home."

"*Hannah.* I still can't believe I—we—have a daughter," Isaac murmured, contemplating the picture on the screen. "Raven's used to feel like home." He looked out the window, and she took in his strong, serious profile, the thick eyelashes she'd enviously teased him about. His downturned mouth. Was he thinking of their daughter?

"You were always welcome here."

He faced her, cynicism twisting his features. "Not everyone felt that way."

"I know, and I'm sorry for that. But I did. Wasn't that enough?"

His gaze cut to the floor. "It should've been."

She kneaded her brows with her fingertips. He was right, and regret sat heavy across her shoulders. Dad had never wanted her to marry Isaac. Still, they couldn't live in the past. Their relationship was over, but the friendship they'd shared still connected them. Bonded them forever. Plus, Hannah.

How would her daughter—*their* daughter—react to meeting Isaac for the first time?

Isaac reached over, giving her hand a squeeze.

"I'll do everything in my power to uncover the lies Hugh is telling about you. And keep you safe."

His touch and words sent ribbons of warmth through her. "Thank you. I know you will."

While their lives had changed completely since their divorce, she couldn't deny that Isaac remained the same caring man she'd once loved with all her heart.

The windowpane rattled, and they jumped apart like teenagers caught kissing in the basement. *Stupid.* It was just a furious gale from the blizzard.

Isaac stared hard at the screen. "Okay. Here we go. Your turn." He pushed back from the desk and stood to let her sit in the chair. She pulled up the local area server and worked through the sign-in screens until she reached the admin level.

After typing in the password, she scooted back and rose. "You want to check the emails?"

"Sure."

She returned to the futon but perched on the edge to peer over his shoulder as he clicked through the email server. "There are a couple years of emails."

"Dad hired him two and a half years ago, so we should start there."

He grunted affirmation. At least all their

names were in their email addresses, which made sorting and finding Hugh's emails easier.

"There are hundreds, maybe thousands, of emails." He released a surprised breath. "Hugh was a busy man."

"From the first day he arrived, all he wanted was to turn this place into Holland's Peak. Nothing here was good enough, big enough, exciting enough for him."

Isaac nodded. Holland's Peak was the premier skiing resort in New England, a mecca for the wealthy and talented in the skiing world. The huge property also hosted the last National Skiing Championships and a dozen regional championship events. While Raven's Fun Runs was a favorite with its affordable family amenities, friendly atmosphere and consistent snow from December through April, their resort wasn't linked to many major skiing events. Profits came from family vacations, winter weddings, high school trips and ski retreats, not world-renowned, press-covered sports events.

"Hugh wanted change. It was like he had a plan about remaking this place, and he stuck to it no matter what. I warned Dad, but he ignored it. He felt we needed more help running the resort. Dad wanted upgrades too, but even he didn't realize how much change Hugh intended to make. Or how much it would cost him." Including his health.

"I'm sorry you didn't have a voice in all of this."

Gratitude swelled in her chest. Leave it to Isaac to pinpoint what hurt her the most. She leaned back, resting her head against the cushion. "I keep thinking that this is all a bad dream. That I'll wake up. That Lars isn't d-dead." A knot of emotion clogged her throat. "What if we don't find proof that it *wasn't* me who killed him?"

"We will."

His confident words soothed her. She tilted her face to look at him, a genuine smile forming. "If you hadn't come back… I don't want to think about it."

"Then don't." He met her gaze and returned her smile, his eyes crinkling at the corners. "Get some rest, okay? I'll be at this awhile."

He was right. She needed to try to sleep. *Try* being the important word.

She lay sideways on the couch, her head resting on the pillow she'd carried from Roger's bed. The smell of his aftershave smarted in her nose. Another gust of wind pummeled the cabin, and the walls creaked in protest. She burrowed under the blanket, grateful for shelter and warmth after the brutal hours outside in the blizzard. Grateful for Isaac's unexpected but welcome presence.

Memories unfurled in her mind. Isaac's rough childhood, which he'd reluctantly shared with her years ago. Half siblings sent to foster homes, a dad he met only a handful of times. His mom charged with a crime when he was young, something about a drug bust at her job. If Everly remembered correctly, she'd played a small roll, mostly by coercion, and then someone else had pinned it on her, a coworker who knew she wouldn't have a solid alibi. She'd been charged and spent several years at a women's correctional facility.

Everly's stomach flipped up, then down, threatening to evict the toast from earlier. What if she ended up like Isaac's mom? Away from her child, alone in a cell. Bitter. Hopeless.

"I don't believe this." Isaac's shocked tone pulled her from the frightening thoughts.

Everly sat up, the afghan twisted in her hands. "What is it?"

"Look at this email." He pointed at the screen. "Between Lars and Hugh, dated last fall. That's definitely a threat."

"Hugh threatened Lars? We can use it, then." Her heart beat out a relieved rhythm.

"That's just it. Lars threatened Hugh."

SIX

Isaac rammed a hand through his hair as he read the email aloud. *"You said she wouldn't be involved in this, and now she's right in the middle. I warned you not to bring her into it, and once again you didn't listen. You couldn't stay away. This ends now or I'll make it end."*

Everly catapulted off the futon. "Why would Lars threaten Hugh?"

He held up a hand. "Hold on. There's a few more emails to go through, but this is enough of a threat the authorities need to know."

"But… I can't see Lars actually hurting anyone, Isaac."

"Maybe Hugh stopped him before he could." He scanned the rest of the page, then glanced her way. "Did Lars share his feelings about Hugh with you?"

"Not really." She returned and sank onto the couch. "He'd make comments here and there about all the construction and building upgrades messing up the slopes and bothering the resort patrons. He was frustrated that he got pulled into all that when he just wanted to teach ski lessons. I finally confronted Lars when I found out he'd okayed adding four more chalets to the tune of several hundred thousand dollars. Lars *said* he hadn't wanted to, but my dad and Hugh pushed him to do it. We had an argument about it a couple weeks ago. I told him he and Ingrid brought Hugh on board and it was his fault. I didn't mince words." Regret laced her voice. "I think I even said, 'You dug your own hole, now you have to lie in it.'" She slid her palms over her face.

"You had no idea what would happen, Everly."

She dropped her hands. "I never liked Hugh, but I had no idea he was capable of…this."

"When was this argument with Lars?"

"I don't remember exactly. We met for lunch at Eichhorns, and Hugh had to leave early, of course. He liked to say his piece, then disappear so no one could rebut him. My dad went with him, as usual, leaving me and Lars. We walked over to the main lodge, and that's where we argued."

"About adding the four new chalets?" Isaac asked.

"Yes." Her forehead furled in a thoughtful frown. "There was something else. Hugh wanted to bid on hosting the US Alpine Challenge next winter. My dad and Hugh urged Lars to get onboard, since as head ski instructor he had to."

"But he refused."

She nodded.

He made a mental note of her words. Had Lars's refusal upset Hugh to the point of murder? Didn't seem possible, but yet…who knew with ambitious people? Isaac stretched his arms and leaned back, the chair creaking in protest. The wound on his arm felt better after she cleaned it, but the fact that he'd missed his last tetanus booster nagged like a stone in his sock.

He scrunched forward, scrolling through more of the emails. A lot of it was pricing for the resort upgrades. Some questions about additions. Weekly reminders for meetings. Employees asking for time off. Much of which Hugh cc'd Ted Raven on. Had Ted read them all?

Realization nipped him. "There aren't a lot of direct emails from Hugh to your dad and vice versa."

"No, they texted a lot. Or Hugh called him. He'd call my dad late at night. Never left him alone. I think that's partly why Dad's health deteriorated the past few months. Hugh's like a bulldog about what he wants."

No kidding. "They were together a lot, then?"

"All the time."

The thought of standing face-to-face with Ted Raven and his cynical gaze sent a swell of trepidation over Isaac, despite having survived training that'd make other men weep. He was no longer an insecure teen or a cocky young adult now, but the older man had always had this way of making Isaac feel less than—in skiing, in his relationship with Everly, in his efforts to finish college and then when he and Everly got engaged. None of Isaac's efforts had been good enough for Ted Raven.

Still, he or Dan needed to interview Ted about his relationships with Hugh and Lars. Soon.

Isaac snapped a few pictures of the emails on the computer screen and sent them to Dan. Would the pictures bounce back? He gnawed the inside of his cheek, waiting. After several seconds, no bounce back message appeared. Good. It appeared the pictures went through. And Roger's extra cable had given them the chance to charge their phones. Hopefully reception improved once the blizzard let up.

He fought a yawn as he rose, careful to position himself next to the window instead of in front of it. He needed to get some shut-eye tonight before they set out in the morning, and so did she. He just didn't want to let her out of his sight.

She jerked into a sitting position. "Alpine's up."

On the floor below, the dog's nails clicked in a rapid pattern. Then the husky bounded up the stairs and beelined for Everly, her low, prolonged whine prickling the hairs on Isaac's neck.

She slid to her knees, hugging the dog. "What is it, girl?"

He crawled to the window. A dark four-door pickup fitted with a snowplow navigated Roger's winding driveway. "Roger drives a truck, you said?"

"Yes, a white Ford."

"Someone's coming and it isn't Roger." One of Hugh's men? They had two, maybe three minutes. She'd cleaned up and put away all the food items in the kitchen, and tossed the first aid items in the bathroom. At least they'd locked the doors and hidden their coats and boots in the double drawers below the futon. Now they had to hide themselves and an antsy dog before the men burst into the cabin and Hugh got what he wanted.

All of them, dead.

Everly's muscles spasmed with adrenaline as she scurried to the stairs. Was there a closet or room downstairs the men wouldn't see?

Isaac poked the power button on the computer

and snatched his phone before scrambling after her. They flew down the narrow staircase, and Everly uttered a prayer of thanks that Isaac had been smart about keeping all the lights off except the porch light, just as Roger had.

Nothing out of the ordinary, he'd explained earlier.

He slinked against the back wall of the living room, drawing her against him. "Is there a crawl space or back door?"

Everly inhaled through her nose. This wasn't happening. "Yes, but... I c-can't." Headlights stretched through the window, and she moaned. "Can't we hide somewhere else? The shed?"

"They'll check the shed. I know this'll be hard for you. But our daughter needs us. Where's the access for the crawl space?"

"In here." She motioned at the kitchen and tried to move, but her limbs felt like concrete blocks. Ever since that avalanche when she was younger, she'd hated being enclosed in tight spaces. "Beneath the rug in front of the pantry."

Isaac let go of her and rushed into the kitchen. He kicked the large, frayed rug away, revealing a rectangle cut cleanly into the wood floors. Fingering the inset handle, he turned and lifted the large opening to Roger's crawl space.

Everly sucked air into her cheeks, then forced it out. She'd seen Roger go down for supplies but had never ventured into the inky shadows herself. Her breath came in starts and stops at what they had to do. At where they had to hide.

"It'll be okay." Isaac motioned her closer. "I'm here."

Everly darted over to him, keeping low. Her legs wobbled on the flimsy stairs descending into the dark, cold tomb. A band of anxiety buckled her chest, tightening with each step down. The crawl space's low ceiling was strung with cobwebs that shimmered in the weak light spilling over from the kitchen. A damp, earthy smell of old things and dirt filled her nose. Something skittered on the floor—a rat?—and Everly bit back a squeal.

"Get Alpine. I have to shut the door."

Her dog paced at the top of the stairs like she didn't want to go into the underground space either. Everly shaped her lips and pushed out a weak whistle. "Come here, girl."

The nervous click, click, click of her nails was the only answer. What if she didn't listen?

"Alpine, come."

Alpine whined, cocking her head. Then she took off from the top step, leaped the half-dozen steps and slid across the dirty floor to land at Everly's feet.

"Good girl." She shoved her fingers through

Alpine's fur as Isaac inched back up the stairs to close the crawl space opening.

Seconds later the meager light disappeared, throwing an ebony blanket over them. She couldn't catch her breath as the dark smothered her, the walls closing in. "Isaac. Did you get the rug?"

"I got it." His hand found hers in the dark.

"I can't breathe."

"Yes, you can. I hear you breathing. Breathe in, count to three, then release. Do it again."

She listened to his voice and did what he said. And it worked, until the slam of a car door carried in from outside, and the swift crunch of footsteps wrecked her focus. The front porch stairs groaned from the weight of someone approaching.

"I c-can't stand this."

"You're a Raven. You can do this."

"But…the avalanche," she whispered.

"It's over. You made it out. Just like we'll make it out of this." He settled an arm around her shoulders, face inches from her ear.

An impatient knock resounded above. "Anyone here?" A man's voice. "Maple Creek PD, I'm coming in."

Everly flinched, and the muscles in Isaac's arm flexed. "The door's locked," he whispered.

"He'll have to break in. I'd alert him to our presence but I don't know who to trust at this point."

"The key! I p-put it in my coat pocket." Everly pressed her fist to her chest. "What if the officer knows it's supposed to be there and it's not?"

A deafening crack shook the structure, and dust drifted into their eyes and hair.

"Broke the lock," Isaac murmured.

Her heart pounded so fast it felt like it would fly out of her body and give away their location. Isaac shifted his feet, and she leaned deeper into him, hating her claustrophobia and the way it made her feel so weak and helpless.

The crawl space wasn't as small as some she'd seen in people's attics or basements, but it didn't matter. Didn't help. The confining walls and low ceiling drudged up memories of the hour she spent trapped under tons of snow let loose after an avalanche. She'd been blinded by white and numb all over, counting her too-rapid breaths because she'd been told the air would run out within thirty minutes and then she would die.

Footsteps circled the floor above, and Alpine whined at her feet. The officer was in the kitchen. The crawl space ceiling shook as the person walked over where they hid, and the bifold pantry door gave a swift creak. Had Isaac placed the rug over the opening well enough?

The man's voice filtered through the floorboards. "Yeah, it's me. They're not here."

Everly cocked her head to catch the conversation.

"Yeah, I checked the closets. No shoes or coats. If they stopped here, they're gone now."

Several seconds passed, and the man lingered in the same spot. Everly's jaw ached from grinding her back teeth, and both of them craned to hear the man's words.

"It's snowing. Their tracks are long gone. Maybe they went somewhere else. No doubt she knows these mountains well. She'd know where to hide." He paused for several moments. "I'll keep checking around here. Okay. Just let me know what you find."

Everly pressed her fingers to her mouth. Familiarity nagged her. Whose voice was that?

The man shifted position. "The owner isn't happy we had to check his house. I think Mr. Dailey is friends with Ms. Raven." A pause. "Of course, I called him. We have to go about this as aboveboard as possible. Keep it clean."

Everly's hand dropped, and she pressed her mouth close to Isaac's ear. "It's the detective. Mark Savage." Her legs quaked, muscles pained from tensing them. Detective Savage was a long-time Maple Creek resident. He and his family visited Raven's in the summer to use the Ropes Course and go hiking. "Could he be w-working with Hugh?"

He shook his head, one finger over his lips. He hadn't answered her question. Did that mean he was thinking the same thing?

Detective Savage continued speaking. "That's right. When I find her, you'll be the first to know. You just do your part. We'll get this done quick and clean." A radio crackled to life. "Got another call. I'll update you later if I get her." There was a loud click. "Savage here."

A garbled woman's voice spilled into the cabin. "Detective? There's been a ten-sixty-two at an apartment complex in town…"

Everly worked her hands into a knot. What did that mean? And what if it was at her place? Hannah. She started to pull away, but Isaac's arm tightened as though he needed to lean on her as much as she needed him to keep her calm.

The dispatcher's voice faded as the police detective moved away from the kitchen. Toward the door?

"Ten four." His words were loud and clipped.

The man lumbered to the door, a key chain clanking with each step. When the door slammed, Everly pushed off the wall.

"What is a ten-sixty-two?" She barely contained her shrill voice to a whisper.

It took several beats before he answered. "It's a break-in at a residence."

"What if it was mine and—" Her words swallowed up in a sob. "What if they have Hannah?"

Isaac shoved a thermos, two packages of crackers and a half-eaten bag of jerky in the compartment below the massive four-wheeler's steering handle. The shed door hung open, bumping the side wall from the blizzard's last bout of wrathful wind. At least the snow seemed to be letting up. His muscles bunched from apprehension and impatience. With phone reception gone again, there was no way to reach Dan and ensure Hannah was okay.

Please, God, keep Hannah safe.

Everly's shocking admission yesterday still struck the deepest part of him each time he considered it. He'd figured his secret, the fact they were still married, would surprise Everly, but her news surpassed his by far. *A daughter.* Part him, part Everly, a precious life he'd had no idea existed. Doubt molded his brow into a frown. Had Everly really tried to contact him, and would knowing about Hannah have changed what happened in his life? In their lives?

Isaac shook off the thoughts. He couldn't change anything now. Only from this day forward. Time to focus on what was ahead. He wasn't certain how long the drive to Fall Line Road—the center of the resort—would take on the recreational vehicle. *Too long.* Likely it would be slow going with the snow as deep as it was. But it was the best plan B he could come up with. Sunrise was minutes away, the lingering storm still insulating them from daybreak's looming arrival.

A deafening burst of wind rattled the roof. He adjusted his ski mask, and the material caught on the stubble on his cheek. At least they had warm clothes. They'd raided Roger's stash, and while most of the winter clothes were too big for Everly, in layers they worked well enough.

The worry returned, nearly pitching him to his knees.

Hannah...in Hugh's clutches. Never had he felt such an all-consuming desperation to reach someone, to protect them. Too much of the mountain separated him from his daughter and his ability to keep her safe.

He sank to his heels to tighten his boot laces. Alpine nosed around the perimeter of the shed, her tail high as she satisfied her canine curiosity. *She's like a cat*, Everly murmured late last night before she fell asleep on the couch. He'd wanted to leave immediately, then realized that wouldn't be safe without a reliable vehicle. No way could they take off in the dead of night in a blizzard. They'd clashed once about it, and he'd paced the cabin as she slept, checking and rechecking reception.

Nothing.

"Everly," he called. She'd gone back inside to leave a note for Roger in his Bible and make sure no other sign of them remained.

She appeared moments later at the front door, bundled so much she looked like a padded, cartoon version of her slender self. Alpine trotted over to greet her, and snow blustered in between them so that he could barely meet Everly's eyes until she was a few feet away. Which didn't matter, because he knew what he'd see.

Fear. Worry. The same emotions that had settled like a block of bricks on his lungs. "You up for driving this?" He pointed to the camo-colored four-wheeler.

"I can drive." Everly stroked Alpine's back over and over. "What if he already has her?"

The bricks pressed harder. "I doubt Hugh would take that great of a risk. Stealing a child isn't his usual MO. He's trying to stay under the radar." *Please, God, let that be true.*

"Did you ever reach your friend again?"

"No." His head fell forward. He'd texted and called Dan numerous times after the detective left. All to no avail. Reception had dropped off again late last night. He'd almost chucked his phone into a snowbank beside the porch when he couldn't get through. "Reception's still out."

"I wonder if another tower got damaged in the blizzard."

The choking sense of helplessness that had plagued him since childhood returned like a blow from a broken tree limb. They had to make it to the center of the resort alive. He had to see his daughter, to hold her. If only there weren't an unstable killer and snowy mountains in their way. He squared his shoulders and took in their surroundings. Winter engulfed the valley, beautiful but deadly. The landscape rose steeply behind the cabin, peaking into a pair of mountains that bordered the main lodging area in the town center. In order to get back to the center of Raven's, they'd have to either go around the base of the mountains or make their way over them.

"How far are we from Fall Line Road?"

"If we stay on the service road, it's just under two miles." Everly tucked her gloves under the jacket sleeves, her face averted. "Off road the distance is shorter, but it's over mountain and could take longer."

She was referring to the terrain, treacherous enough on its own. Add limited visibility, massive snowdrifts and possible avalanches? It meant disaster.

"I say we stay off the road. We've got the best

ATV driver around." He winked at her, and her eyes widened before she looked away.

He'd lived for teasing her when they were younger and married. But now...was it too much?

He handed her a pair of black ski goggles he'd found in the shed. "Let's go."

She dropped into the front position, tugging them over her ski cap. He climbed on the back so they sat snug on the seat. The strap of his goggles rubbed his skull, but he ignored the friction.

Alpine yipped up ahead, then dashed off into the snow, full of energy. Isaac almost chuckled. At least one of them was having fun.

"You sure she doesn't want to get on the rack back here?" He motioned behind him.

"She's fed and full of it. If she gets tired, I'll make her get on." Everly gave a thumbs-up and revved the engine. She gunned the throttle, and they sped away from the cabin. Isaac secured an arm around her waist and fell into the vehicle's choppy, rocking rhythm. When the wheels caught on an icy spot, she slowed, giving it time to grip, then continued with a determined grunt. She knew what to do on black ice.

Everly edged the base of the mountain, Alpine loping nearby, nose to the wind.

Isaac turned. Roger's cabin shrank into a

speck in the distance. "Let me know if you want me to drive."

She pulled slightly away from him. "I got it."

And she did. She always did. A blast of reality thumped him, harder than the wind. She'd always been fine on her own. Without him. She needed him now because her life and freedom were on the line.

He'd always felt like an imposter at Raven's. With the added wisdom of a few years under his belt, Isaac couldn't blame Ted Raven for his concerns about how he was raised, although the man had never chosen to get to know him or give him a chance to prove himself either. It was for the best that their marriage had ended, and once this mess was over, they'd make sure that was finalized and figure out a schedule so he could become part of Hannah's life.

A tiny black dot broke through the swirling storm clouds to the east, and his heart crashed into his ribs.

"Everly, it's a chopper! Go left! Into those trees!"

SEVEN

Everly wrenched the handlebars left as the helicopter closed in. They were being hunted from the sky now too? Her heartbeat roared in her ears and her senses blurred as though everything moved in slow motion.

"There! See the rocks?" Isaac bracketed her with his arms, his hands covering hers to help her steer. An uneven wall of boulders flanked by snow-capped evergreen trees snagged her eye as they guided the four-wheeler sharply left while maintaining speed.

The vehicle spun on ice and slowed, and Everly jogged the throttle until it caught solid snow and momentum again. Had they been spotted?

She glanced back as the helicopter sliced through the sky toward them. It disappeared in the low storm clouds, then reappeared. Larger. Closer.

They were turning too fast. Isaac's chest

pressed into her back as he reached to take control, cutting the throttle. He slammed the brake with his long legs, then jerked the wheel, jogging the four-wheeler ninety degrees. Everly screamed. They fishtailed, sliding toward the rock at an alarming speed. She clenched her eyes shut as they stopped just short of the boulder.

"Back it up," said Isaac.

She flipped it to Reverse, turned the throttle and guided it with his help beneath a short evergreen. Snow plopped onto their shoulders and the branches enveloped them. Finally, the world stilled. Everly worked to calm her explosive breathing, then whistled for Alpine. The dog wove through the low branches and slid in next to them, prancing in uneasy circles as the whomp, whomp of the helicopter grew louder.

"Sit. Stay, girl." They made it. *Thank You, God.*

Isaac leaped off, positioning stray branches over the shiny metal and shoving the four-wheeler deeper into the foliage. Was the brown-and-green off-road vehicle camouflaged enough? A clump of snow splattered onto her head when Isaac tugged her off the seat at the base of the tree.

"We have to be ready to run in case they see the ATV."

She nodded, settling an arm around Alpine. Wind swirled the loose snow around them, shaping it into a tiny tornado. Overhead, the helicopter's buzzing increased, then decreased as it circled the area in wide loops.

"How are they flying in this?" Isaac glared through the branches.

"Hugh must've gotten a local pilot. They're used to performing rescues in this type of weather." Still, it carried a dangerous risk to fly in a blizzard, even one that was dying down. *Speaking of...* Fear coiled in her throat, and she closed her eyes. "Will they see our tracks?"

"Doubt it. The snow's still coming down enough that our tracks should be covered." But his voice held a hollow ring.

Her daughter's cherubic face filled the dark space behind her eyelids. The thought of anything happening to Hannah created an avalanche of panic that buried all other rational thought. How could she protect her daughter in all this?

"What if—what if once we get to the resort center, I turn myself in to the Maple Creek police."

He turned to stare at her. "You'd likely end up with Detective Savage. Do you really trust him after what we heard at Roger's?"

"I don't know." She tucked her chin so he wouldn't see the truth in her eyes, that she'd wondered the same thing about the detective, especially after what they overheard last night. "I can't imagine he'd get involved with—"

"Start imagining it."

"Why? His parents, he and his wife and kids are longtime resort patrons. They always seemed like good people."

"Money changes people. Desperation does too. Happened to me. I went after that stupid story in La Plagne for the chance at the big time. We don't know that Savage isn't doing the same."

"You loved to chase stories, Isaac. Loved discovering hidden truth through interviews. That's why you majored in journalism and psychology."

"We're not discussing me, Everly. We're talking about you and how to keep you safe."

"Fine. But I still think it's worth a try to turn myself in—"

"No. I'm not willing to take that risk until I figure out what Hugh's angle is in all this. What I do know is he wants you badly enough to blow up a chalet and go out into a blizzard to get to you." He flicked out bits of snow caught in the pockets of his coat. "I have a feeling that Hugh and whoever he's working with want you out of the picture, with all the blame on your shoulders."

Black dots fringed her vision. *Out of the picture.*

"Please, Everly, let me make sure it's safe first." Isaac's dark brown eyes narrowed, head cocking as he listened. "The chopper's coming back this way."

She flinched at the thunderous whir roaring overhead, and beside her Alpine trembled, whining at the oppressive noise. The tree bowed under the gusts, its branches flattening to the earth. Shoving and scraping them. Through the swaying branches, a black-clad figure caught her eye. Leaning from the side of the helicopter, the man held a long black gun pointed their way from directly over them.

Her heart floundered. It was the man Alpine had attacked.

Isaac tugged her closer to the trunk of the tree. Speaking now was impossible with the deafening whir of the helicopter's blades. A prayer filled her mind, the one she'd read over and over when she was a child and young teenager and her mom still took her to church. Before Mom's cancer diagnosis and Everly's crisis of faith. *I will say of the Lord, He is my refuge and my fortress: my God; in Him I will trust. Surely He shall deliver thee from the snare of the fowler and from the noisome pestilence.* Everly's legs sank deeper into the snow, her nerves throbbing with each turn of the rotors. The earth vibrated.

The helicopter rose, circling higher in the stormy sky, increasing in radius until it no longer flew directly over them. The figure remained fixed in the window, a sliver of black gun glinting. When the machine tucked its nose into the wind and took off toward Maple Creek, Everly's muscles loosened into a puddle of relief.

Isaac drew himself to a standing position, bringing her upright with him. "I don't think they saw us that time."

That time. How much longer could they elude the men? Between finding Lars dead, Isaac's sudden appearance, the man chasing them through the pit, getting shot at in Isaac's truck and now being harassed by a helicopter, Everly's fear for Hannah and herself—and Isaac—quadrupled. She shoved at the branches with a righteous anger. "What does Hugh want?"

Isaac worked the four-wheeler out from under the tree. "Could be his desire is for complete control of this place. And unfortunately, you're standing in the way of that."

Everly adjusted her goggles. Alpine trailed after them with her tail between her legs from the helicopter's racket. Everly stroked the dog's head and scratched her ears, then they mounted the ATV, Isaac's face aimed at the sky.

"You really don't know why all of this is happening?" She swiveled on the seat.

"Not yet." His expression turned to flint. "One thing I do know? He wants you dead."

Isaac nudged Everly. "We've got to get moving. Do you want me to drive?"

"I got it." She started the four-wheeler and maneuvered them from the hiding spot like a pro. Alpine lay across the rack on the back, and he sat half-turned, one arm over the dog so she was secure. When Everly increased the speed, flecks of snow dumped on them by the tree flew off as they raced away. He tightened his hold on Alpine, his mind as wired up as the athletic dog's body.

Abbot had been located. That had been him hanging out of the chopper like a stuntman. Hugh must've put some kind of tracking device on his men. And now Hugh knew Everly had help.

They hit a bump, jostling sideways, and Alpine shifted with a yelp. He adjusted his arms as his thoughts dialed back to Detective Savage and his appearance last night. Who was he really working for—the local police force, or Hugh?

Isaac made a mental note to have Dan check the man's record at the local PD.

As for Everly, he had to convince her that turning herself into Maple Creek PD wasn't a good idea. That it would play her right into Hugh's hands—which would sign her death certificate. Isaac had a feeling Detective Savage was dirty, and until he knew otherwise, it was his job to keep her alive and away from Hugh. Her strong will and intelligence had always appealed to him, but now they threatened her life.

"Are we staying off the service road?" he shouted over the wind and engine.

"For now."

What did that mean? Going near the road was too risky. "Everly?"

"Just trust me."

He did, but now? With their lives at stake, and the skies beginning to clear, danger was coming at them from all sides. He clamped his mouth shut as they skirted the base of the first mountain, trailing to the far side to keep under the cover of the trees. Broken branches from the storm stuck out of the snow like wooden arms reaching for rescue from the frozen depths.

He scoped out the sky. Remnants of the blizzard remained in the straggling clouds cocooning the mountaintop. Random gusts of wind tugged at their clothes, and snow floated haphazardly about, no longer driven to the ground like last night.

Which meant Hugh and his men would be out in force now.

Hannah.

Isaac closed his eyes for a moment. How was it possible to love someone you'd never met, never talked to, never even seen? And now he'd do everything in his power to keep her mom safe and, hopefully, meet her one day soon. What about Everly? With the divorce not valid, would she ever...

He ground his jaw. Everly was done with him, at least romantically. The divorce paperwork snafu was a clerical error, one that could be righted with the swipe of a pen. While his heart might want to play that "what if" game, his head told him to connect with their daughter, build a relationship with her, but leave Everly well enough alone. Ted Raven had made it clear she was better off without him, and Isaac recognized that to be the truth. He'd just have to prove the man wrong about being a loving father to Hannah.

The dog wiggled beneath his hold. "I think she wants off."

Everly nodded her okay and slowed the fourwheeler.

He released his arm, and the dog leaped off in a perfect arc, landed nearby and trotted up the slope.

Everly increased the speed. "I can't stop thinking about Hannah. Worrying about her."

So, this was what being a parent was like. "Me either. I've been praying nonstop that she's safe."

"God and I haven't really been on speaking terms for a while," she murmured. "But all I can do is plead with Him for her safety."

He squeezed her shoulder. "I'm sorry to hear that. Funny thing is I *started* speaking to Him."

"When?"

"After my accident."

The curve of her back straightened. Was she hurt by this news? Or surprised? "You didn't seem interested in faith or God when we were younger."

Isaac blinked through the hazy regret that clouded his vision. "I was stupid. About a lot of things." He ignored his jumpy nerves and asked something that had nagged him since he found out about Hannah. "How did your dad handle the news that…you were expecting?"

"He wasn't happy about it at first," she whispered, and he had to lean forward to catch her words. "Once Hannah was born, he forgot about his dislike of…our situation and fell for his granddaughter. She calls him Poppy." She began the slow ascent up the backside of the mountain. Isaac pressed into her as the wheels dug for traction on the snowy, steep incline.

Poppy. Isaac had a difficult time picturing the astute businessman crouching to speak with a little girl, but maybe having a granddaughter had softened Ted Raven.

A cloud passed over his thoughts, and in its absence, a startling realization dawned.

"You said your dad has been sick a lot. Is there a diagnosis?"

"Not so far."

"When did that start?"

She steered the ATV right, avoiding a narrow ravine. "A couple years ago, but he's gotten a lot worse the last few months."

Hugh Markham had come on staff about the time his health tanked. Could be a coincidence, could be stress. But what if it was something more disturbing than that?

Isaac eyed the woods surrounding them and debated telling her his theory. "Ted—your dad—was in good shape before that, right? Jogged on the treadmill and golfed in the summer?"

"Mmm-hmm," she said. "But he's lost weight recently and hasn't skied for a while. The treadmill is in my apartment now." She slowed the four-wheeler as they neared the peak, and he kept his gaze on the sky as they hit open ground atop the mountain. Far below lay Raven Valley, dotted with lodges, condo units, and resort amenities interspersed with a mini-golf area and a ropes course for summer patrons. Plus, Eichhorns restaurant and a few new buildings Isaac didn't recognize. They were tiny in the distance, still a mile or so away, but at least they'd make it in the next couple of hours.

She drove the four-wheeler slowly across the peak, likely searching for a trail leading into the woods. Good. They needed to descend ASAP, but also under cover. Alpine scampered nearby, her pink lolling tongue making her easy to spot.

"Did he start getting sick *after* Hugh arrived?"

Her body tensed. "Yes. You think the stress from Hugh and all of his demands made my dad sick?"

"No. I wonder if Hugh is poisoning him."

Everly pressed the brakes into a hard stop and whipped around, the green flecks in her eyes highlighted by surprise. "How would he do that?"

"I'm not sure. But that paperwork in my truck? I've been going over those files for several days, looking at the last decade of Hugh's life. Markham has left strange carnage in his wake—people end up sick." *And dead.*

Everly narrowed her eyes. "So, you do work for the police."

"Not—"

A silver speck burst through the clouds strung across Raven Valley.

The helicopter was back.

"Everly, go!"

Not again! Everly twisted the handlebar and revved the ATV's engine. It shot forward with a growl, kicking up snow in its wake. She forgot to breathe as the chopper made its way toward them like a huge, deadly insect.

A dozen yards from the woods, the four-wheeler's speed increased—too much. Her shriek cut the air as she lost control. Isaac wrapped his arms around her and dove to the side, sending them tumbling to the snow as the vehicle careened sideways toward a wall of trees.

They rolled downhill in a painful pile of limbs and boots. Isaac grunted as her elbow caught his chin, and his boot jammed into her calve. With each roll Everly saw the four-wheeler's crash like it was in slow motion. It smacked into a tree trunk, then spun and rolled into the woods, metal parts flying off, embedding in the snow a few feet from them.

She clenched her eyes shut and braced for impact. But the strong bands of Isaac's arms found her again, and the spinning sensation slowed. Then stopped. They landed a couple of feet from the crunched ATV, the buzz of the approaching helicopter filling their ears.

They were under the cover of trees, but the shiny metal of the crash would catch the pilot's eye. Or Abbot's. Dread twisted her stomach. Where was Alpine? At least she hadn't been riding with them when they crashed. Everly tried to whistle, but only a sputter of air came out. Her pulse pumped blood through her temples as the whirring noise increased.

Isaac grasped her shoulders, rotating their bodies so they slid on their backs deeper under the trees. "We need to get under cover." His voice wavered, his body shuddering with each turn.

She gasped. Blood saturated Isaac's sleeve. "Your arm!"

"It just…reopened. I'll be okay."

A soft ringing caught her attention. She tilted her head, and clumps of snow stole down her neck, leaving cold trails under her jacket as she tried to locate where the noise was coming from. It sounded like a cell phone.

"That's me," Isaac murmured. "Must have…

reception." He squirmed, searching his coat pockets for his phone. The helicopter hung overhead, blasting the trees with wind.

"I don't know where Alpine is!" Everly turned, squinting into the sky. "What—that looks like a different helicopter."

Could Isaac call for help before they were caught? Her eyes prickled. *Please, God.* Once she'd worried about Hannah never knowing her dad. She'd wondered if she should pay an investigator to find Isaac, to let him know about his child. Now the thought of her daughter being so close to meeting Isaac and these men stopping that caused a flood of sorrow to choke her.

Alpine burst from the bushes behind them and loped over. She nudged her head under Everly's arm, burying it. The poor dog hated the sound of the chopper too.

Isaac let out a strange sound, like a gurgling laugh.

"What is it?" Was his wound getting worse?

"That one is for us." His dark eyes smiled at her, and Everly's chest constricted at his expression of relief. He rested his forehead to hers briefly, then exhaled. "You're safe."

Safe? She pulled away and glanced down the mountain, where the helicopter now hovered over the emergency pad at the edge of Raven Valley. "What's going on? Who is that?"

"It's Dan. He found a pilot and secured a chopper."

"Who's Dan?"

"He's my superior. I mean—" he gulped, his face a mixture of pained grimace and gratitude "—we work together...for the FBI."

"What?"

Alpine whined after her surprised exclamation. Shock and incredulity created starbursts in her peripheral vision. *This* was what he'd been doing since he asked for a divorce and disappeared?

EIGHT

Everly sidled up to Isaac in front of the wind-cleared landing pad, her heart a frightened bird inside her chest. She held Alpine's collar firmly. The silver-and-blue helicopter sat like a moveable metal tomb, its blades slowing. But inside were friends. Allies. Isaac's partner was on their side.

His partner in the FBI. Everly turned her head, pressing her cheek to her shoulder as Isaac's words raced across her mind like a level nine skier on a black-diamond trail. He'd briefly explained it was best for her to know as little as possible about Hugh's case, and that was why he hadn't told her initially. For her safety. The surprising announcement almost made her forget she was about to get into a helicopter.

She'd ridden in one once—the day she'd been rescued from the avalanche. Her anxiety spiked, but she slowed her breathing and squared her shoulders. Now they could get to Hannah faster, and Isaac would get the medical help he needed. Plus, they could track down the evidence to prove her innocence.

She could do this.

A tall, silver-haired man stepped out of the helicopter as they approached. His lanky stride and intent expression seemed vaguely familiar. "Isaac. Glad you two—" he shot a surprised look at Alpine "—you three made it out of that blizzard all right."

Isaac strode closer, and the two men shared a firm handshake. "Dan."

Dan inspected Isaac's sleeve. "It looks like that might sting a bit. I've got something inside the chopper for that." Then he removed his sunglasses and assessed Everly with direct blue eyes that struck a déjà-vu chord. Where had she seen him before? He crossed his arms. "Ms. Raven. Are you ready to get this misunderstanding sorted out?"

"Yes, but first I need to know if my daughter is okay."

"She is," he said, the words an instant balm to her fears. "One of my men is set up near your apartment." The man's sharp gaze cut to Isaac. "The break-in that occurred last night happened on the other side of that neighborhood—an empty rental apartment, apparently."

"An attempt to flush Everly out."

"Most likely," Dan agreed. "But still, there's the question of her guilt."

"I didn't kill anyone, if that's what you're implying," Everly spoke up. "I have no idea how that bloody shirt got in my office."

"Did you go back in your office after you discovered Lars Henken's body that day?"

She hesitated, glancing at Isaac. "Yes. But my dad was with me, and a couple other employees came in. We were all crying. Upset."

"Understandable. We'll take your sworn statement soon." He glanced at Alpine. "Is the dog friendly?"

"If you're not a threat," Isaac volunteered with a chuckle.

"She'll be fine." She bent to murmur, "stay" to the dog, then took Dan's offered hand. As she let go, recognition flared. "We've met before."

"That's right. You might remember my daughter?"

Everly racked her memory. *Williams...* "Are you Lizzie's dad?"

"That's correct. Lizzie's my youngest." Dan turned toward the chopper.

Everly blinked at this revelation. Lizzie had been a gangly downhiller—a junior national silver medalist—with an easy smile who'd torn her ACL a few years ago. She'd finished college and become a physical therapist, turning her tragedy to triumph. If Dan was Lizzie's dad, then trusting him wouldn't be so hard after all.

"The dog comes along." Isaac scratched Alpine's ears, then looked Everly's way. "You ready?" He pressed his palm to the small of Everly's back, and they climbed aboard.

There were two seats beside the doors, and a third bucket seat caught her eye behind them. Away from the windows. Everly pulled in a haggard breath and sank onto the creased leather. Alpine jumped inside and beelined for Everly, lying underneath her feet.

She tugged off her gloves and hat and ran a hand through her hair. She must look a straggly mess.

Dan and Isaac took the other seats, engrossed in a conversation she couldn't quite catch. Isaac slipped two small objects to Dan, then took the medical kit Dan offered him.

What had he given him? The key and note?

Everly's phone chimed in her coat pocket. She pulled it out. Reception at last. Numerous texts filled the screen, covering her home-screen picture of Hannah's sweet face, which was a tiny replica of Isaac's except with Everly's nose. Tears seared her eyes. Once this awful mess was over, Everly needed a long tickle hug with Hannah, a hot shower and eight hours of sleep.

And, she acknowledged grudgingly, time to

talk to Isaac about their past. While he wasn't husband material, so far, he'd proven he could be a trustworthy father to Hannah.

The pilot began flipping switches until the engine turned over, blades rotating above them. Alpine yelped at the noise, setting her head on Everly's shoe. She stroked Alpine's neck, understanding the dog's concern about this form of transportation. With each click and jerk of metal, her fatigued muscles tensed up. Outside, the blizzard sputtered its dying breath. Weak gusts of wind nudged the helicopter's attempt to come back to life.

"You okay?" Isaac pivoted to face her as they lurched slightly forward, then rose, the sensation sending her stomach into her mouth. He'd removed his coat and wrapped gauze tightly around the cut.

"Slightly better than I was up there. Are you okay?"

"Definitely better." He tucked his wounded arm to his side.

She pointed a shaky finger toward the peak where the four-wheeler had crashed and remained. In pieces. "Roger's going to kill me."

"I wouldn't worry about that right now," Isaac said.

Dan cut in. "From my earlier conversation with him, Roger seemed legitimately concerned about your safety. I'm fairly certain he'll be glad you're out of danger."

Was she out of danger?

She flicked her gaze to Dan, who was perusing two files. "So, where's Hugh?"

Dan didn't look up when he answered. "My source said Hugh is taking Ingrid to her sister's in Boston. I have word that he won't return until this evening at the earliest."

"What about the men working with him?" Isaac inquired. "We haven't seen them since their helicopter took off. Any idea where they went?"

"I have a man posted at the gas station near the entrance to Raven's. Said the chopper headed back to Maple Creek not long ago. There's a helicopter service based out—"

"Stan's Scenic Tours," she provided.

"Right." Dan dipped his chin then continued. "Now, about what I found. I pulled info on Hugh from the database I'd like to go over."

"Wait." She lifted her hand from Alpine's head. "How did you two even meet?" Isaac worked for the FBI. The knowledge still felt like a puzzle piece that didn't quite fit in her brain.

Isaac shot a questioning look at Dan. The older man raised his wiry gray brows, then returned his attention to the files in his lap. "Go ahead."

"Dan and I connected after my accident. He's familiar with the skiing world because of his daughter but works for the FBI. He was in France with Lizzie for the same competition when I—when I hit that tree. He saw it all. He came to the hospital to check on me later, we talked, and…that eventually led me to give the FBI training academy a try. To work with him."

The chopper rocked sideways like a dangling Christmas ornament batted by a cat. Everly sucked in quick, tiny breaths, attempting to focus on Isaac's explanation and not the closed-in, moving metal box powered by paper-thin blades they were flying in. Alpine whined from the floor, inching closer.

"Dan and I are part of a new FBI task force monitoring corruption in professional sports. My sports journalism reputation was a great cover. We work in tandem with local law enforcement, and since Hugh's case crossed state lines, here we are."

"It does seem like the perfect fit for you." Admiration bloomed in her chest. It felt as though everything she knew about Isaac had been wiped away like marker on a white board, and he'd stepped into a new identity. What would her dad say if he knew how Isaac had turned around his life?

Dan waved his phone. "Excellent. Hugh's

former coworker at the Park City resort agreed to testify."

Isaac made a victorious sound. "That'll nudge the DA to reopen the case, then. Maybe reexamine evidence."

"Let's hope. That's the goal." Dan handed Isaac a file, a loose piece of paper sitting atop it. "Look at this. Specifically, the names."

Isaac went silent as he read the offered page. His head jerked up, and he turned to face Everly. "Did Lars ever talk about how he knew Hugh before he recommended hiring him?"

"No, not to me. But the skiing world isn't huge, so no one questioned their relationship."

Isaac held out the paperwork. "Looks like they co-owned a business years ago."

Everly snatched it, devouring the print on the decades-old document.

R. Hugh Markham and Lars H. Henken, co-owners, No-Fall Ski Rentals. Anderson Circle, Park City, UT.

She met Isaac's eyes. "I knew Lars and Ingrid met and married in Park City, but we had no idea Hugh and Lars ran a business together."

"Your dad didn't know?"

"I don't think so." Doubt wound around her tongue. "He never mentioned it."

Dan cleared his throat. "I'll dig deeper into that connection. Isaac, you mentioned the name Bobby several times. You believe this man is working with Hugh, correct?"

"Yes." Isaac ran his hand through his hair, and Everly's fingers twitched as the wayward locks stuck up in all directions. Once she'd enjoyed fixing his thick brown hair, but now—that was in the past. She massaged her temple to erase the absurd thoughts.

Isaac handed the paper back to Dan, and the older agent's gaze jumped to her. "Ms. Raven."

"Yes?" She sat up straight, feeling for all the world like she was still in elementary school and the principal had just admonished her.

"There's one more thing you need to know. I received news an hour ago that your father is at Maple Creek Hospital."

Her stomach dropped despite the helicopter remaining steady in the air. "Dad's back in the hospital?" Was it from stress and worry about the murder investigation—or from poison, like Isaac believed?

"I have a man at the hospital keeping an eye on his room."

"Is he okay?"

"He was discovered this morning in his home, passed out. Blood pressure was extremely low, and last I heard he was in ICU."

"I need to see him."

Isaac's features pinched into a scowl. "Not a good idea, Everly."

"Please. I'll be safe with you there." She shifted her gaze to Dan. "Seeing me may improve my dad's condition."

Dan tugged his ear and scowled as Isaac mumbled something under his breath. Finally, the older man motioned at Isaac. "I have a car. You take Everly into town so she can see her dad. A quick visit. Then we'll track down a judge to sign off on the search warrant."

"Yes, sir."

"Thank you." Relief was a short-lived gift as she looked into Isaac's tense face and flatlining mouth. What could go wrong at the hospital?

Isaac shut the SUV's front passenger door and jogged around the car. He folded himself inside and buckled the seat belt, glancing Everly's way. She'd been silent since they exited the chopper and handed Alpine off to Dan to bring to Sheila, a longtime Raven's employee who ran Eichhorns Meats and Eats.

He turned the ignition. "Hey, you okay?"

"Yes. No. I don't know." Her eyes met his but slid away, returning to Dan's vehicle as it made its way toward the restaurant where Alpine would wait for them until they returned. "Do you think my *dad* will be okay?"

"I don't know. Dan didn't have much information about his condition." He released his death grip on the steering wheel to set one hand on her knee briefly. "I hope so." For Everly's sake. For the sake of their resort. Even for their daughter's sake, as it sounded like she adored her *Poppy*.

Isaac withdrew his hand. It burned him that Ted Raven had been the sole male influence in his daughter's life because *he'd* been absent. Much like his own dad. But that would be changing.

He jerked the car into Reverse, then Drive, guiding it out along Fall Line Road. At least the plows had come through to clear the roads. Trees blurred out the windows, capped in white and weighted by snow. German-style lodges crowded the main road, light tan and white with brown roofs and brown accents. Smoke swirled from the main lodge and a couple of other buildings, including Eichhorns. Bittersweet nostalgia washed over him. In the summer, green blanketed the landscape, but in the winter the structures Everly's grandfather built were perfectly set in their element, hearkening back to a German village.

They sat in silence for most of the ten-minute drive, until they crossed into Maple Creek's city limits and he asked for directions to the hospital. He could've used his GPS but wanted to drum up conversation again. Instead, Everly directed him the right way and went back to staring out the window, showing him her profile and remaining quiet.

Was she upset about the fact that he worked for the FBI now, or just worried about her dad? He'd kept his position under wraps because Dan believed it would protect Everly. Now, Isaac wasn't so sure. Maybe it would've been smarter to share the details right away so they were on equal ground. After all, secrets always had a way of biting the hands of the one who held them.

Speaking of secrets. He rolled his shoulders as guilt about their unfinished divorce paperwork twisted his nerves. Now wasn't a good time, though. Clearly her mind was elsewhere.

They rolled through light traffic on Maple Drive, the main road cutting through the small city. Visitors thronged in front of Gondola Gifts, and a line curled out from Blizzard Brews. He kept one eye on the road in front and one behind them, but so far the only threat came from bored tourists, who'd spilled into town when Raven's closed, running across the road.

When they pulled in to the hospital lot, he parked away from the other vehicles and scrutinized the surroundings. Only a few cars of note—one white cargo van with a hospital logo on the side and a police cruiser idling at the ER entrance. A black truck beside a mini-van. Otherwise, the unassuming brick hospital sat quiet. Isaac let out a loaded breath. Could it be that Hugh really had cleared out of town? What about his men, though? Either way, he wasn't letting his guard down.

"Ready to see your dad?"

"More than ready." She released her seat belt, but Isaac threw his arm out to stop her.

"Hold up. Let me go first."

Isaac scanned the lot once more, then climbed out, came around and opened Everly's door. They hurried toward the hospital's sliding doors.

"Let me do the talking," he said, brushing her arm with his. The front desk was quiet, and the receptionist directed them to the third floor without looking up from her computer.

At the elevator, he slowed. "Do you want me to stay outside his room?"

She turned to face him, her features a study in barely controlled tension. The urge to wrap his arms around her hit him hard, but they weren't out in the storm any longer, and she likely wouldn't appreciate the gesture. "You don't want to see my dad."

He didn't bother denying his discomfort about

seeing Ted Raven again, sick or not. "I'm here for your support. That's it."

She gazed at him for several seconds. "And for my protection."

He nodded, drowning in the hazel depths of her eyes. But he broke off the connection because he needed to focus and shut down that foolish part of his heart that still held out hope.

"If it's okay, I'd like you to come inside."

"I can do that." If Ted Raven didn't mind, at least.

Suddenly her eyes widened at something she saw behind him, and she dove forward, into the embrace he'd just longed for. His arms automatically wrapped around her back, and hers came around his middle, her face nestled into the fabric of his coat. He ignored the electric thudding of his heart and bent his neck to speak in her ear. "What is it?"

"Behind you. I think that's Ingrid. I... I can't deal with her right now."

So, she was hiding. His body hummed with adrenaline, and he edged his face sideways to scan the situation. A couple walked out of the hospital, backs to him and Everly. A woman and a man. The woman's short white-blond hair and designer ski coat caught his eye, and slowly he turned them around, keeping Everly and her identity in the safety of his arms. The pair headed left and disappeared from sight. Which car had they driven—or was Hugh picking them up?

"Are you two on bad terms?" he asked into her cheek.

Everly pulled away from him. "Not really bad terms. She's just a lot to take. There's always drama and everything is about her, you know? I just can't handle it right now."

"She changed her hair." When he'd met her, years ago, it'd been long and dark. "Does it make sense that she would've come here to visit your dad?"

She tilted her head back and forth, considering. "I guess so. It just seems…strange with Lars gone, that she would do that. But she and my dad have known each other a long time, so…" She raised a shoulder. "Maybe it's nothing."

He wasn't sure about that. Especially since Dan had gotten word that Ingrid was going to her sister's with Hugh. Which meant Hugh wasn't out of town. A frustrated sound very much like one of Alpine's growls rumbled in his chest.

"Come on." He pulled her into the elevator. "Let's get this over with and get you back to Raven's ASAP."

They stood apart as the elevator dinged shut

and rose three floors. Once they exited, he located the room numbers and headed straight for 310. A plainclothes officer sat in one of the waiting-room chairs, flipping through a magazine. The man didn't look up when Isaac and Everly passed, instead setting two fingers on his knee as a silent acknowledgement. Everly didn't seem to notice, and they continued toward Ted's room.

The door was open, and a petite nurse trotted past just as they arrived.

"You're here to see Mr. Raven?"

"Yes, we're family." He spoke before Everly could, and she nodded, her slender form trembling slightly and leaning against his. In his peripheral vision, he could see her dad laying in the hospital bed, the TV on in the background like a buzzing insect.

Painful snippets of the time he spent in the French hospital after his accident flashed through Isaac's mind—Ted Raven coming and going in his room, giving Isaac an earful when he was barely conscious. Isaac flexed his jaw, pushing back the uncomfortable memories. He set his palm on the small of her back and guided her toward what felt way too much like a firing squad inquisition.

NINE

Everly gulped down a sob. Her dad leaned back on his hospital bed, weariness lining his face, the grayish pallor of his skin shocking. The hospital gown dwarfed his tall, bony frame like a tablecloth, and the sharp point of one elbow stuck out from the blanket. She tempered her surprise and worry, falling to her knees beside his bed.

"Dad, I'm so sorry you had to come back here."

"I'm fine. Already feeling better, in fact. What is *he* doing here?" Dad's hazel eyes—the same shade as hers—narrowed at the sight of Isaac standing stoically behind her.

"He brought me here to see you." She stroked his embattled arm strung with IVs and beeping machines monitoring his vitals. "I can't believe this. What happened?"

"I wasn't feeling well. Ended up on the bathroom floor." He waved his free arm, scowling. "I'll be fine. Just need to eat more."

Clearly it was much more than that ravaging his body. "Have you found anything out? Do the doctors know what's causing this?"

"Well, they know it's not cancer." For a brief moment, her dad's indomitable confidence wavered as he spoke aloud one of the few words that rendered him powerless. The disease that had taken his wife, Everly's mom.

"I'm so glad." She set her hand over his.

"And, they're pricking me left and right. I'm surprised there's any blood left in my body. One of them even asked me if I've ingested any chemicals lately? I told him Sheila's coffee might pass for a chemical, strong as it is." He chuckled.

Chemicals. Everly shot a glance at Isaac, but he hovered in the doorway, monitoring the hall.

Dad continued. "They did chest X-rays and scanned my brain." He dropped his chin in one of his classic get-down-to-business gestures. "Now why don't you explain to me why *he's* back in Maple Creek?"

An odd look passed over Dad's face. Fear?

She glanced around at Isaac again. He'd moved and stood near the counter, reading something on its surface. His features were inscrutable as his eyes roved over the paperwork.

In the background, the commercial cut to the local news.

Everly spoke loudly to combat the news anchor's baritone reporting. "Isaac is in town working on…a story."

"A story? About Ravens?"

"Yes. Sort of." She grabbed at what information she could share. "He's the one who kept me alive when we were lost in that blizzard."

"So, you didn't run away on purpose?" Dad used his thumb and pointer finger to massage his forehead. "Savage made it sound suspicious."

Detective Savage. "No. Well, yes I ran, because someone—Hugh—sent men after me. With guns, Dad. They chased me down Tipping Point last night."

"What—why would Hugh do that?" The machine beside her dad's bed clicked, then beeped loudly as though in warning.

"I—I mean, we—don't know that yet. Isaac and I are trying to—"

Isaac cleared his throat loudly. She pinched her lips and exhaled in small bursts. Hint taken. She couldn't tell her dad anymore about Isaac's role in this. On the TV, a blonde reporter took over from the desk anchor, her strident words thundering through the room.

"The investigation continues at Maple Creek's

popular ski resort, Raven's Fun Runs. And now sources are confirming that Everly Raven is considered a person of interest in the murder of international skiing star and beloved local ski instructor Lars Henken. Sources also confirm that the building in which Mr. Henken's body was discovered burned yesterday afternoon in what officials are calling a 'highly suspicious' incident. More on that in the afternoon update."

Everly turned to Isaac, drawing her hands up, crisscrossing them over her chest. He'd moved away from the counter, closer to her, his features made of stone as his thumbs jabbed his cell screen in rapid strokes. She angled back around and dropped her arms, meeting her dad's incredulous expression.

"Everly." He coughed, the raspy sound matching her faltering heartbeat. Constant beeping filled the room, and Dad let out a groan. "Tell me…it's not…you."

She gripped the edge of the bed. "Of course not."

The nurse hurried through the doorway, checking the machines and inspecting her dad. "Let's keep this low-key. Mr. Raven is pretty weak. Don't want him upset right now."

"I'm fine," Dad bellowed.

"You are not," the nurse shot back, clearly

used to his belligerent personality. She set his chart on the counter with a clatter.

They bickered for a minute, and Everly inched backward out of the fray, her gaze darting between the television and her ailing dad. If only she could rewind time and undo what had happened. Talk to Lars, tell him to ski on a different slope that morning.

She set a curled fist to her mouth. "I can't believe this."

"I can." Isaac jammed his phone back into his coat pocket.

"Can they arrest me?"

"Not yet, but local authorities want to get you in for questioning soon. And I have new information."

"What is it?"

"Not now. Let's wrap this up and get back to Raven's."

Her hand brushed his as she shuffled sideways to whisper, "I'm sorry my dad's being so rude."

"No worries. Your dad berating me in a hospital room? Nothing new here."

She slit him a look. "What do you mean?"

He lifted one shoulder in a shrug. "Just get as much info out of him as you can without talking too much about what happened to you. That's what will upset him the most. He loves you. Tell him something that'll make him feel better."

She nodded, caught between these two men she loved—no, one she loved and one she once loved. What had her dad said to Isaac after his accident in France?

She returned to Dad's bedside after the nurse left.

"How's my baby girl?" Dad asked, referring to Hannah. Again, he shot a worried look at Isaac, like his presence was more than an irritant. Like it was a threat.

"She's safe with Becca, at my apartment." She motioned at her ex-husband. "Isaac made sure they posted a guard at my complex."

Dad grunted his surprise. "Did he, now? Does he also plan on filing for custody after this mess is cleared up?"

Custody? Everly's breath snagged in her throat.

"No, sir, I don't plan on trying to take Hannah—*my* daughter—away from *your* daughter. That would be incredibly selfish, and I don't have that in me to do."

Silence reigned in the room, and Dad's brows slowly sank from their raised position.

"I'd like to begin a relationship with my daughter, not take her away from her mother.

I have no doubt Everly—" he coughed slightly "—and you have done a great job raising her."

Warmth bloomed in Everly's chest at Isaac's conciliatory words.

"Yes, well, I'm not sure that's best for Hannah."

"Of course, it is, Daddy. I want Hannah to meet Isaac. To get to know her dad."

Dad laid his head on the pillow, eyes closing. "I think I need to rest."

She twined her fingers, concern drilling a hole through her middle. Should they not have come here? "Okay, we'll head out, then. I'm…" It was her turn to clear her throat. "I'm praying for you, Dad."

He mumbled a response she couldn't make out, then turned his head, facing the window. The nurse puttered in, hands filled with medical gadgets and medication.

"He really needs to sleep now."

Everly nodded, tears prickling her eyes. She leaned closer and pressed a kiss to her dad's cool cheek, then hurried over to Isaac. He filled the doorway, peering down the length of the corridor.

"Ready?" he inquired.

She nodded, following him. They traced their steps and neared the elevator. The hallway throbbed with a strange silence that sent chill bumps along her limbs. Isaac froze, scowling at the empty waiting area, eyeing the length of the hallway.

"Isaac?" Her arm pressed into his.

"The guard is gone."

Just then a man wearing a green baseball cap and brown leather jacket emerged from a room down the hall opposite her dad's, his face in shadow, chest rising and falling rapidly.

Blood trickled from his nose like he'd just been punched. She swallowed a scream as the man spun in their direction and jogged toward them.

Isaac threw himself between her and the threat. "The stairs, behind you! Go!"

When Everly whipped around to run, she caught a glimpse of the lone nurse, hurrying from behind the desk. But the man shoved around her, sending her clipboard flying and the nurse staggering back. Everly accelerated into a sprint.

Isaac rode her heels, his body in between her and the man like a human shield. The slap of their pursuer's shoes on linoleum burned her ears as she ran for the stairwell door. She reached it, shoving it open, pounding down the concrete stairs.

They descended the levels in dizzying turns. One more level. Her heartrate skyrocketed as a metal door smacked the wall somewhere above them. The man was in the stairwell too.

Finally, the first level door. Isaac burst past her, his weapon drawn and features taut with concentration.

He pushed open the door, eyed the first-floor hallway, then pulled her through.

"Stay with me." They dashed across the lobby.

"I'm trying!" Her tongue stuck to the roof of her mouth and her chest heaved with exertion.

"Excuse me, what are you doing?" the receptionist called out as they sailed past.

"Call the police." Isaac tossed the words back. "There's been a fight on the third floor. There's a man down."

They shot out the main doors, and again Isaac drew them to a stop, his head swiveling side to side. Then he took off, tugging Everly across the hospital parking lot. Isaac loaded her in the passenger door first, then circled the vehicle and leapt in. As they drove away, his eyes were glued to the rearview mirror.

"Take Old Hollow Road. It's a side road no one knows about. Gets us back to Raven's faster." Everly pointed, gripping the seat belt.

They headed down Old Hollow Road, Isaac driving nearly twice the speed limit. Adrenaline sizzled through her veins like a hot caffeinated beverage. Maple Lake stretched out to her right, hidden beneath a cover of ice and snow.

"Is the guy following us?" She peered in the side mirror.

"Not yet."

Not yet? A dull ringing filled her ears. "My dad…what if that man tries to go after him?"

Isaac tightened his grip on the steering wheel until his knuckles turned white. "My gut tells me that guy was after you, not your dad. Can you grab my phone?" She tugged his cell from his pocket and tried to hold it steady as he sailed down the winding road. "My code is 0606. Dan's number should be the most recent one—"

She swallowed a sudden lump of emotion—*0606?* His phone code was her birthday month and day? No time to consider that now. "What do I say to him?"

"Pull up his number—whoa! Here he comes. Everly, brace yourself!" Isaac shouted as a black truck filled the side mirror, the same man they'd seen in the hospital in the driver's seat.

"Isaac!" Everly exclaimed, his cell phone flying out of her hand and across the dashboard.

The truck bashed into the SUV's fender, sending their vehicle careening sideways on the snow-edged road.

The lake.

Everly screamed, and Isaac wrestled with the

steering wheel as the SUV fishtailed, everything around them blurring in an icy maze of white and black danger.

"Hold on!" Isaac held his hands steady as the SUV slid sideways off the road. *The lake.* He muscled the skidding vehicle, riding the brakes carefully and attempting to aim for the trees instead of—

The SUV brushed against a tree, and he gritted his jaw at the impact and metallic crunch. A side mirror swiped off, ripped away by the tree trunk. But the tree barely slowed their momentum, and the vehicle slid the rest of the way toward the ice. The front end dipped low as the ground inclined into the frozen tomb below. In his peripheral vision, he saw the black truck take off down the road, shrinking in the distance.

He couldn't think about that right now. *Please, God, keep us off that lake.*

"Isaac!" Everly screeched as their vehicle crept onto the ice. "Should we—"

"Get in the back!" He unbuckled her seat belt, pushing her into the back seat. The front tires slid easily, with nothing to catch on the slick surface. Would the trunk open from the inside? Isaac's breath raged as he directed her farther back, to the third row of seats.

Would the ice hold? Or was the weight of the vehicle too much? The front end dropped suddenly, and the sound of sloshing water sent a ripple of fear through him. The engine was going under.

"Here! The button." He lunged across the narrow space to poke the square black button. The trunk lid rose, revealing the vehicle was fully on the iced-over lake, stopped only because the front end had broken through and now settled deeper and deeper in frigid waters.

"Everly, go, go!" He thrust her toward the open trunk as he climbed across the seats. "Jump across!" Motioning, he positioned his legs to help propel her crouched form farther. After securing his hands on her back, he shoved with all his strength. She leaped across, the motion similar to Alpine's graceful movements, and landed on the snowy bank. She made it. Dizzying relief coursed through his limbs.

The SUV pitched toward vertical just then, plummeting farther into the lake.

Freezing water trickled in, lapping at his boots as he scrambled to the edge of the trunk and set his heels on the plastic liner, gathering energy before shoving off with all his strength.

The doomed vehicle offered only wobbly ground, sinking farther as he hurtled up and away. He threw his arms out, reaching for dry land, anything to grab onto, as he landed on the edge of the lake's surface. Pain zigzagged across his shoulder and into his scalp from the barbed wire wound. The trail of broken ice from their vehicle bumped and sloshed around him, icy water enveloping his feet and lower legs as he landed a couple of feet away from the edge.

"Isaac!" Everly's cry matched the desperation buzzing in his ears. His boots kicked out as numbing water soaked into his pants. Then—there! The lake bottom. Shallow ground.

Thank You, God.

"Here! Grab this!" Everly held a thick branch out to him. He snagged it, careful not to pull her toward him instead. Seconds later he stumbled onto the ground next to her. She wrapped her arms around him, sobbing. He sat up, setting her slightly away so she wouldn't get cold lake water on her too.

"You're going to f-freeze."

"I've never been so happy to roll in the snow." After checking that his Glock was secure and dry in its holster, he reached for his cell in his pocket. Empty.

He groaned. "My cell." The evidence they needed now rested below the ice.

"You mean this?" She tugged the small black device out of her coat and presented it to him with wobbly hands. "It slid back my way and I grabbed it."

Without thought, he enfolded her in a tight hug. She stiffened, then relaxed in the embrace. "Nice job, Raven. There's evidence on this." He dropped his arms. "Sorry about that."

"It's okay," she whispered.

He thumbed through to Dan's number as they clambered up the incline to the road so she wouldn't see the heat staining his cheeks.

Everly's elbow scored his ribs as she swept around. "Do you hear that?"

The rumble of a truck engine burdened his ears. No. Not again. He analyzed the area. Nothing but road and trees and snow surrounded them now—and ice. On foot, they had little chance of getting away.

"I think that's Roger!" Everly pointed. A white F-250 approached, a plow raised along its front bumper, a scowling bearded man driving.

The truck pulled up beside them. "Everly Raven, what are you doing out here?" Roger's gruff, incredulous gaze shifted to Isaac, his frown deepening. "Isaac Rhodes, that you?"

"It's me."

"Looks like you two need a ride."

"Yes, please," Everly murmured. "We need to get back to Eichhorns." She traced around the bed of the truck to the passenger door. Isaac followed, keeping an eye on the road in case the black truck reappeared.

Inside the cab, he started a text to Dan, detailing all he could remember about the truck and what had happened. No sign of the vehicle that had run them off the road, but Isaac had a sinking sensation that it wasn't the last they'd see of the man.

TEN

Everly gripped the mug, tremors of shock kindling beneath her skin despite the warmth of the restaurant and the hot drink. She couldn't stop picturing Isaac in the back of the SUV as the lake claimed the vehicle with deadly, icy liquid fingers. Who had run them off the road—another of Hugh's men?

Now that she was a person of interest in this case, would she ever be free from the chains of doubt in the Maple Creek community? She sipped the coffee as her mind strayed again to Isaac. After Roger dropped them off, her ex-husband had entered the back-apartment area of Eichhorns, greeting Sheila with a lengthy hug, then downing the coffee she set in his hand. He'd asked about a shower and disappeared without another word.

Sheila wobbled over, the coffeepot like an extension of her arm. "Top you off, hon?"

"No, thank you." Adding more caffeine to her

system would only amp up her jumpy, sleep-deprived heart. Her gaze crossed the room to Alpine, resting on her lumpy bed in the corner. Everly worked up a weak smile. Her dog was well-fed here, no doubt. Sheila didn't let any-one out of her sight without a full belly and a breath-squeezing hug. Including dogs.

"I can't believe someone tried to run you off the road," Sheila sputtered as she retreated to the stove, where she set the coffeepot down with a clatter. Her childhood in South Carolina often appeared in a thick Southern accent when she was upset or stressed. "God was watching over you, hon."

"Yeah, I guess He was." Saying the words aloud knitted together the fragile pieces of her fractured faith. "Thanks for letting us come here."

"You are welcome here anytime."

"Even when I'm a person of interest in a mur-der case?" The words tasted bitterer than black coffee.

"Never mind what you heard on the TV. Hugh's acting like you're dangerous. You, of all people!" A cabinet door slammed as the older woman rifled through cookie sheets. "We need more rolls."

Everly blinked at the far wall, where match-ing portraits of pigs dressed as a farmer and his wife hung beside the window. The pictures usually made her smile, but not today. Today it felt as though she were a wild animal in the woods. Hunted and alone.

No, that wasn't true. She wasn't alone. Isaac was here, and the truth of who he was now—an FBI agent—washed over her like the wind from last night's blizzard.

Sheila returned and set two buttery rolls in front of her. "Your daddy texted me earlier. From the hospital. Teddy asked me to keep an eye out for you." She puffed her chest out. "Sometimes I wonder about that man—and I'm sorry, I know he's your daddy—but he sure doesn't make the best decisions. He needs people at his side he can trust."

"He's been so sick I doubt he's thinking clearly." For months she'd believed Dad was stressed about the resort, but now? Now it appeared Isaac was right about someone poisoning him. Especially after what her dad said about the doctors' questions.

Everly considered her and Isaac's brief time at the hospital. "Have you seen Ingrid?"

Sheila swiped at the perspiration beading her brow. "Not today. Yesterday she came in for dinner. In between tears, she mentioned that Hugh might be taking her to her sister's today."

Everly shifted her feet beneath the table. Did

Ingrid believe she had something to do with Lars's death? "She must be devastated about Lars."

"Devastated." Sheila wiped her hands on her apron. "Right."

Everly schooled her features to hide her surprise. Why did Sheila say it like that? Was there bad blood between the women, and Everly had never noticed?

Footsteps resounded on the stairwell down the hall. *Isaac.*

"Everly. Sheila. Did I miss anything?" He strode over and sat at the table beside Everly.

"Just us talking about how Hugh's blaming Everly." Sheila faced Isaac. "I just can't get over you, young man. All grown up. Fighting the bad guys like one of the actors on *NYPD Blue*."

His mouth curved in a humble smile. "Not quite."

"I sure would've liked to hear how you were doing these past few years," Sheila gently admonished him.

"I know. I'm sorry, and I…" He angled his face toward the ground before raising it. "I regret the way things happened."

"Well, you're here now, and that's what matters." Sheila set a pair of rolls in front of him then circled back to the oven.

Everly glanced at Isaac as he downed more

coffee and popped them into his mouth. He caught her look, one corner of his mouth rising in a questioning expression. What was wrong with her? She pushed away from the table to give him space and get her head settled.

"Hold the phone," Sheila wheezed from behind Everly. "Does Isaac know about...?"

She beelined for the sink then turned. "I told him about Hannah."

Sheila's smile lit up the room like a hundred-watt bulb. "She's precious, Isaac. You will absolutely love her. My favorite little customer."

"I already do." His dark eyes found and clung to Everly's. "If that's possible."

"Well, of course it is." Sheila sighed. "It's wonderful to see you back here, in good health too. My heart about broke into bits after your accident and then finding out that you two were getting a divorce."

The finality of that word hardened Everly's resolve to clear her mind of fanciful thoughts of her ex. She faced the sink, twisting the faucet until hot water gushed over the dirty mug and her fingers.

"About that," Isaac murmured deep in his chest. "We were *supposed* to get divorced."

Everly whipped around, water droplets spraying the room. "What did you say?"

"The divorce didn't, um, officially go through."

She gripped the sides of the sink. "How— Why— When did you—"

"The lawyer forgot to mail the final documents after the six-month separation period ended. I was in training at that point, missed the email and never knew to check back with him."

She clenched her eyes shut, then reopened them to find him watching her. "We're not officially divorced?"

"No."

A log slipped in the fireplace, the sizzling pops entering the conversation like exclamation marks. Everly's mind clung to his admission but couldn't quite grasp its reality.

They were still married.

She'd have to go through that pain all over again? It was too much.

Sheila broke the stunned silence. "What a week this is turning out to be!" She scurried to the oven, hauling out another tray laden with rolls. After topping the steaming knots of bread with a dab of honey, she slipped half of them into a wicker basket. The homey scent tantalized Everly's nose and stomach. "Still married. Mercy. And all I can do about any of it is feed people. Someone needs to eat these sweet rolls. Isaac?"

Isaac slipped three from the basket and popped them into his mouth in rapid succession. Everly stood like a statue, her muscles as uncooperative as her brain.

They were still married...

Everly tried to move, but all she could do was watch as Sheila made her way around the kitchen area, cleaning and coaxing more food into Isaac's hands.

"I have some beef stew left over from yesterday. You kids want a bowl?"

"I'd be glad to relieve you of some of that stew," Isaac said. "Thank you."

"You got it, darlin'." Sheila hustled into the heart of the kitchen, and the clanks of pots and pans followed. Everly made her way back to the table, measuring her steps and thoughts.

Isaac watched her approach, his steady appraisal sending an army of goose bumps over her skin. She pictured the determination on his face as he shoved her into the trunk of the SUV, his strength as he pressed her to safety and then thought of himself.

"You should probably shower and get changed." Color flared on his cheeks. "I mean, you look fine. You're good, it's just..."

"I know what you mean. I will in a few minutes." A flurry of questions converged in her thoughts. "How long have you known we're still married?"

"A couple months. I felt the same way you do now. Couldn't believe it."

"It's unexpected, that's for sure."

"I'm sorry I'm just telling you now. I hated to drop this bomb right away though, with all that's happened. Getting that email kind of felt like…"

"Like you were being forced to confront a part of your past you didn't want to?"

"Yeah, pretty much." Isaac tipped his head back, weariness stamping his features. "I would've told you right away, but I didn't want to dump more stress on you."

"I get it. We'll work it out, right?" Which was what she wanted…wasn't it?

"Right. I'll get the paperwork from the lawyer as soon as we clear your name and you're off the hook. I promise."

Why did his honorable tone unleash such conflicting emotions inside her? Everly ignored all of them and focused on one. Gratitude. She leaned over and pressed a kiss to his cheek. "Thank you for rescuing me from that lake."

"Anytime." His throat bobbed in a swallow. "That's why I'm here."

She settled back in the chair, a blush heating her neck and cheeks from her impulsive actions. A quick peek his way showed Isaac's mouth pulled in a severe line, eyes downcast.

"Isaac, what is it?"

He took several seconds to answer. "I found out something at the hospital, when I looked over your dad's chart."

The tender feelings that had blossomed moments ago crumbled at his hesitant, chilling words.

"They have him on fomepizole." Isaac held her gaze. "Normally they do that treatment if they believe someone ingested antifreeze."

Isaac waited at the bottom of the stairs in the back of Eichhorns as Everly descended. "Once it's dark, we're going to Lars's townhouse. I'd rather you not come along, but right now there's no choice. You're not staying here without protection."

She gripped the railing. "You're not in charge of me."

"No, I'm not. And I don't want to be. You're an independent, capable woman who doesn't need m—doesn't need help—except right now." He reached back, massaging the stress knotting his neck. Maybe he'd phrased his dislike of this situation, of having her tag along while he searched for evidence, poorly. "Right now, I'm trying to keep the mother of my child safe."

Her frown smoothed out, until her mouth quivered and a light shimmered in her eyes.

Tears? She looked away before he had a chance to analyze it more.

Alpine trotted down the hall, nails clicking on the wood floor. She nudged up to Isaac, and Isaac bent down, scratching behind the dog's ears and along her back until one hind leg twitched.

"You figured out her favorite spot." Everly giggled, the soft sound a welcome reprieve after the moments of tense silence between them. She took the last step to stand beside him, joining in on petting Alpine. "You're staying here, girl."

He straightened. "When we get there, I need you to do what I ask. For this case and for myself, I can't stand the thought of you getting hurt."

"I will." She licked her lips, and Isaac wrenched his gaze from the movement. "And... I understand. You want to keep me safe for Hannah's sake. I feel the same. I mean, it would be awful if you were hurt, or worse, before you even met her."

He gave a nod, the emotional cord of their daughter's life binding them tightly together. He pushed all those new feelings aside and dialed back to last night and the ranger station. The message had read *825 Mogul Lane. Finish by midnight 1/18.*

"Hugh found Abbot and likely figured out

we picked up the dispatch and key. Hopefully, we delayed them some. Dan obtained a search warrant and gave me twenty-four hours to track down the evidence we need to clear you."

A half an hour later, pitch black enveloped them as they darted around the restaurant. Streetlights arched over Fall Line Road, creating an eerie glow above the pavement. Clouds hid the moon and blocked out the stars, and the bitterly cold air snuck under his gloves and hat and made his lungs ache.

"Good to go?" he asked Everly.

She gave a thumbs-up, and they took off. Using a vehicle at this hour was a dead giveaway, so on foot it had to be. Lars and Ingrid's townhouse sat approximately eight hundred yards down the road. He'd mapped it on his phone before leaving and monitored the road. No sign of Abbot and Eddy.

Yet.

Dashing from tree to tree still left them in the open more than was prudent. At least the pain reliever Shelia gave him remedied the ache from the arm wound, which had reopened during their lake incident.

He slowed, dropping into a crouch. "You okay?"

"Never better," she answered, clouds bursting from her quick breaths.

He stayed put for several seconds to let her rest. Isaac adjusted the ski mask and catalogued the past twenty-four hours. Sheila, Everly's dad, Roger—Isaac believed all three were innocent of any wrongdoing against Lars and certainly against Everly. They all loved and cared for Everly. That much was abundantly clear. She was a part of their circle here, a beloved member of the Raven resort community.

But him? Shunned by Ted, questioned by a skeptical Roger and scolded by motherly Sheila. Confirmation that Everly didn't need him in her life.

He ground his jaw. "Ready?"

"Just go. I'll keep up."

There was the Everly he remembered. Spunky, always up for a challenge. Isaac set off in a stooping run with her right on his heels. He slowed at the next stop—a five-foot metal mailbox that resort customers used to mail items while staying on the property.

Only one more section of the resort blocked their path now. Isaac drew in a frosty breath. The Packed Powder Putt-Putt Park. The distant rumble of a car sawed clear through his focus.

"It could be them! Come on!" He vaulted the four-foot fence, then swerved through the odd-shaped greens covered by tarps and blanketed by snow and ice. Everly scrambled over.

A vehicle approached from the direction they were headed, driving noticeably slower than the speed limit of twenty-five. They huddled together in the dark as the crunch of tires on snow neared.

Everly leaned into Isaac as the car passed by, then slowly disappeared. Had the men already been to Lars's place?

He listened for several moments before motioning her on. "They're gone. Let's move."

A giant statue of a skier on a slope was the focal point of the park. He pushed off the edge of a concrete fountain and veered around a huge fake toboggan that sat overtop the final, most difficult hole on the course. The fountain was silent, water long shut off. Everly tailed him through it all.

Isaac climbed over the fence on the other side, waited for her to do the same, then shot across the last stretch of land. Then down the hill past a small park that separated the commercial and residential areas of town. The dark shadow of the townhouse community appeared castle-like compared to the mini-golf course, the white and brown buildings set in close blocks and surrounded by a ten-foot wrought iron gate.

He approached the gates and trailed around to the back of the buildings. The ground crunched under their shoes, the snow slippery and uneven.

A door slammed in the distance, and Isaac whipped around, eyes narrowed and a hand on his Glock.

"Who was that?" She fell in beside him.

They were too far from Eichhorns to hear a door shutting at the restaurant. No movement within eyeshot. Was the noise from here or another part of the resort—like over at the main lodge?

"Not sure." Once he was satisfied that they weren't walking into a trap or being watched, he gave her a thumbs-up. "I think it's clear."

She pointed at the gate. "Try the eleventh panel. It was loose, and there's a work order to fix it."

He counted them off then wrapped his gloves around the bars on the eleventh panel, shoving with his boot. The lower right-hand corner groaned in protest but held firm. Had someone already fixed it?

"Maybe like this?" She stepped near him, jimmying the gate with the heels of her gloved hands.

They pushed together, and the panel gave way from the ground, opening just enough for them to wiggle through. She slipped through first and he followed, scrutinizing their surroundings. Every window was dark, most of the curtains drawn. The only pale light radiated from a porch at the end.

"That one is Lars's unit." Everly pointed.

Isaac jogged over to the building, keeping track of Everly's location by her breathing and the swish of her clothes. At the residence he pressed against the wall and peered through the dark. Nothing. He edged toward Lars's front door, hand on his weapon, then motioned Everly after him. They slunk past a prickly holly bush, and he scoped out the area before locating the keypad on Lars's door.

A Christmas wreath still hung on the bloodred door, and *Welcome* was painted across it in wooden letters, the invitation ringing hollow. Isaac had known Lars as an acquaintance and instructor, not quite a friend, as Everly had. He'd been an easygoing man, a patient ski instructor. One of the few who'd seemed to welcome Isaac into the resort fold without judging him, unlike Ted Raven.

What had the man done to get on Hugh Markham's bad side? Told him no one too many times?

Isaac adjusted his black gloves, then tapped the ten-digit master code Everly whispered to him.

The lock clicked, the light blinking green. "We're in." He inspected their surroundings once more before entering the townhouse, Everly right after him.

Stale, cool air hit him right away, and an unpleasant odor smarted his nose as he closed the door and locked it. Everly huddled in the shadows to his right, pressed up against a full coat rack. The lone night-light threw an inverted shadow down the hall outside the kitchen, highlighting the closed doors. Lars must have had an office, and that would be the first place to check for a file or any information on the man's relationship with Hugh.

He tugged off his hat but left his gloves on. A shudder worked its way up his backbone. Lars hadn't been killed here, but Isaac couldn't shake the chilling sense of foreboding within the silent dwelling.

"Wait here."

She gave a shivering nod. He crept deeper into the home, inspecting the first floor before following the staircase up and making sure the second floor was empty. He shoved closets open, then stepped back, hand to his weapon. Nothing.

He doubled back down, drawing Everly from her hiding spot behind the coat rack.

She grabbed hold of his arm. "I can check the bedrooms. See if there's anything in their room."

"Okay. Move quickly and quietly. Don't touch

anything. Let me know if you find anything suspicious. We have to leave everything the way it was. Got it?"

"Yes."

"We're in and out. And keep your gloves on."

She nodded and released his arm with a squeeze, then disappeared in the dark stairwell. He continued through the home. Leather couches, a plush carpet and stark, colorless artwork filled the narrow living room, at odds with what he remembered of Lars's simple, down-to-earth demeanor. Must be Ingrid's taste. Isaac continued, the rank smell now overpowering.

What was it? Had Ingrid not been here for days? He froze midstep in front of the kitchen. Half of the white cabinets were opened, and the high, round table was piled with dishes and paperwork. Were those files? Disappointment burned like acid reflux in his throat. He was too late. The men must've been here. An empty chair sat dead center in the galley kitchen, facing Isaac. A couple of plates were stacked on the counter, half-eaten food on them… Was that chicken left defrosting in the sink?

He would say that Ingrid's grief had kept her from the housework, but this looked like a couple weeks' worth of mess.

There had to be something else. Something other than paperwork tying the men together.

No time to waste. He stole down the hall, past a half-open bathroom door, throwing a glance into the small room before continuing to the last door in the hall. Office or bedroom? He stepped inside, the inky blackness enveloping him.

He pulled out his cell and switched on the phone's light. Office. Searching the desk revealed two drawers that opened easily, but the third was locked. He glanced around. In the spot where a laptop would be, the space was blank. The police probably had it.

The smell of rotting chicken oozed into the room, and he eyed the awards and photographs on the wall to focus on something else.

His gaze traced the framed photos of Lars and Ingrid, skiing. They covered every inch except directly around the window. Some pictures appeared to be from when they were first married, while a few looked like they could've been taken in the last couple of years. Most were older photos, and all were on the slopes, Ingrid beaming on her skis, her hair long and dark the way he remembered. Years ago, Everly told him that Lars and his wife had both qualified for the National Skiing Championships but only Lars had made it to the gold medal round. Isaac stepped closer, squinting. Was that—

Surprise tunneled his vision to one particular picture. A faraway shot of Ingrid, Lars and another man hung high on the wall in the corner. Above his eye level and almost hidden. But it sure looked a lot like—

Hugh.

It was a younger Hugh, but definitely him. Had to be. Maybe twenty-five, thirty years ago, he'd guess. The man in the photo was slimmer, his hair thicker. But the face—Isaac had studied it well before coming to Raven's. He grasped the dusty frame and lifted it off the wall. Maybe the picture had a date, like photos used to when they were developed in stores.

He pulled the back piece from the frame tabs holding the picture in place and slid it away from the frame. The aged picture was curled at the edges and faded. He set it back on the desk and tucked the rest of the frame under his arm. *There.* Under the cell phone light, feminine handwriting caught his eye. Cursive words scrawled across the back in faded blue pen.

Me and Lars with Bobby. Happy one-year anniversary of No-Fall Ski Rentals. Snow Valley Resort, Park City, UT. The year appeared to be in the late 1980s, but it was smudged enough he couldn't make it out.

Bobby? Isaac's jaw unhinged. Had Hugh gone by a different name when he was younger? So, Abbot had been telling the truth, and Hugh Markham had an alter ego.

Unbelievable.

He placed the picture inside a waterproof bag in his coat. Then he set the frame inside one of the desk drawers and rested his hands on the desk. It was likely that Hugh asked his men to break in here to retrieve the paperwork for his and Lars's business venture. No-Fall Ski Rentals. Could that be the reason for the files all over the kitchen? Isaac exhaled a hard breath. Had Dan checked business records for the two men?

His phone dinged. No time to check. He'd look once he was outside.

He dropped and crawled beneath the desk, using the cell phone light to inspect the hidden shelves underneath. Nothing but old skiing magazines and a dusty pencil sharpener.

Above him, everything was silent. No sound of Everly creaking about. A grin loosened the tight line of his mouth. Maybe she would make a crack FBI agent after all. He checked the time on his cell. Five minutes and twenty seconds. He'd planned on them being inside eight minutes, tops. He glared at the empty shelves then backed up. Best move on.

His nerves prickled. Isaac whipped around to find a large shadow filling the doorway. The intruder launched at him, and Isaac tumbled left, his elbow jamming into the filing cabinet. The hard landing dashed the oxygen from his lungs. He calculated the intruder's size and shape as he rolled and leaped to his feet. Not Abbot, who was tall and thin, and not Eddy, whom he'd gotten a glimpse of in the parking lot and who appeared short in stature. Someone else.

"Boss said you'd be hard to kill," the larger man snarled.

"I sure hope so."

A spark of memory ignited before the assailant closed in and threw another jab. Could this be the man Everly said visited Hugh, acting like his bodyguard? And the one who'd chased them from the hospital earlier?

"Hey, James, you up for a tussle?" Isaac growled, ducking away from the punch, twisting to pound the man's back with an uppercut to his lungs. The man grunted but stayed upright, meaty fists swinging.

"How do you—" the man grunted as Isaac landed a jab "—know my name?"

"I know everything about you. I know you need—" he landed a blow to the man's shoulder that sent him reeling "—to stop following us," Isaac shouted, all his thoughts centering on the second floor. *Everly.* Did she hear them?

Please, God, keep her silent.

The assailant matched his quick movements.

They traded jabs, Isaac sidestepping James's efficient uppercuts. No time to grab his gun. The assailant faked a punch, then launched at Isaac, fastening himself to Isaac's upper body. They toppled to the floor, and Isaac twisted out from under him, then reached, flinging the desk chair at the man. Pain radiated up his wounded arm. The intruder pushed the chair away, then rose.

Isaac sprang, feigning high, then aiming low. His arms wrapped the man's midsection, then he swept his dominant leg, sending the man back to the carpet with a thud. Isaac slid up his midsection and flipped, wrapping his legs around the intruder's neck as the man pummeled Isaac's face. Three years of jujitsu paid off.

He squeezed with his thighs, cutting off the man's air. Liquid dripped into Isaac's mouth from one of the punches—blood, likely. He squeezed harder. Ten seconds with no oxygen and he'd have the intruder incapacitated.

"I thought you'd be able to handle this yourself."

Isaac's legs went slack at the second voice. He jerked sideways when another assailant dropped a fist on his temple, the blow stunning him. Stars dotted his vision. He swung out, his jab landing with a satisfying thud in the man's eye socket.

The second intruder's pained howl filled the office.

Something pricked Isaac's shoulder, burning the muscle. He shook free, but it was too late.

He let out a groan as everything went black.

ELEVEN

Everly stood immobilized inside Lars and Ingrid's bedroom, her palm curled around the closet doorknob and feet frozen. Had Isaac moved furniture? Couldn't be. He'd stressed being quiet and not changing anything.

A definite thump followed by the rough tangle of male voices brought her hands to her mouth. Isaac's voice railed loudly, breathless and strained. He was being attacked!

Blood whooshed in her ears. What could she do? She had no weapon, no way to defend herself or Isaac. A resounding thud echoed through the townhouse as though a large object—or person—had just taken a hard fall. She tiptoed to the closet door and slipped inside. Her fingers searched along the wall for any weapon or tool she could use. Nothing but clothes and boxes of shoes and boots. Helplessness choked her.

Please, God, protect him!

The sound of creaking stairs turned her to

stone. Someone was stealing up to the second floor, and trying to be quiet about it. The closet door. It was partially open, and the only thing keeping her safe was the cover of night. If the person came in the bedroom and turned on the closet light, it was over. But all she could think about was Isaac. Was he…dead? It couldn't be. A sob filled her chest, threatening to erupt.

The man who'd come up the stairs entered Lars and Ingrid's bedroom, the swish of his clothes and raspy breath giving away his presence. Sweat trickled down her back from the stuffy air in the closet. *Hannah.* Her poor child couldn't lose both of her parents—in one night.

Flashbacks plagued her as the intruder closed in. Lars's body. The crimson circle haloing his head, the blank look in his eyes. She was next.

Everly's muscles tightened into concrete at the man's proximity. He stood where she'd been standing just moments ago, his heavy breath hammering the closet door.

"Let's get out of here," another man called up the stairwell.

"Not done looking for her."

Everly scored her lower lip with her teeth, digging in until the taste of blood smarted.

"No time. Boss said to take out the FBI guy and get out of here." The intruder downstairs grunted. "There's no sign of her here. Now move!"

"If you woulda done your job at the hospital, I wouldn't even have to look," the man in the bedroom shot back, slamming the closet door the rest of the way shut. Everly quaked like the last fall leaf clinging to a branch in November.

"What'd you say?" the man downstairs asked.

"Nothing. I'm comin', I'm comin'."

Suddenly his footsteps retreated out of the room and back down the hall. Then—the stairs. She released a careful breath into one of the coats, then sank to her backside on the carpeted floor. The shoe rack bumped her hip as she waited.

Isaac. The sob returned, lodging in her windpipe. She waited as long as she could—three minutes from when the men shut the front door and a car engine revved nearby, then drove away.

Everly withdrew from the closet slowly, eyes roving the dark room. She slunk down the hall, her ears tuned in and nerves prickling with awareness. Taking the steps two at a time, she slowed at the bottom, moving forward an inch at a time. What was that sound? Running water? She leaped off the stairs and darted toward the noise.

Her indrawn breath turned to a gasp in the downstairs bathroom.

Isaac lay in the filled bathtub, his arm outstretched over the top of the porcelain. Water soaked the rug and trickled toward the bathroom door. His drenched dark hair stuck up in all directions, head low in the tub.

Swirling water lapped at his neck.

"Isaac!" She rushed forward, shutting the water off. He lay in his clothes, blood crusting his nose just above the waterline and mouth like a red bandana. Had they shoved him under? Tried to drown him? Was he already gone?

She sank to her knees to feel his pulse. Slow but steady. *Thank You, God!*

Everly plunged her hand in to release the drain plug then checked his limbs and torso for gunshot wounds. The water slurped in retreat, and her sprinting heartbeat eased up as she pulled her cell out, flicked on the light and examined him more closely.

No wounds except the re-opened barbed wire cut and a laceration on one cheek. It was swelling, turning purple as she sat there. Leaning down, her ear hovering over his face, Everly drank in the sound of Isaac's shallow but stable breathing. The thought of him dead—gone from her and Hannah's lives forever—cut her deeply. For several bursting moments she didn't care about Hugh. Didn't care what happened to Lars's investigation or the evidence they were seeking. Simple gratitude burned behind her eyes because Isaac was still alive.

Was it just gratitude?

Everly shuddered, then sat up, blinking away the tears. Now wasn't the time to consider her feelings toward Isaac. She had to get them out of here. With Isaac soaked, it wasn't safe to go outside. They had to find clothes for him or he'd freeze in minutes.

A racking cough shook Isaac's frame, and she knelt beside him.

"Isaac. I'm here."

Another moan, eyelids fluttering. His features screwed up in a pained frown.

She snagged a hand towel from the wall rack and wiped his face and brows. "Can you talk?"

"You…leave…might come…back."

"I'm not going anywhere." She finished drying his neck and ears with the towel as the water drained, then finger-combed his wet hair, ignoring the fact that she was doing it to comfort herself as much as to comfort him. "We need to get you up."

Teeth clenched, she slipped her arms underneath his and thrust him upright in the back of the shower. He'd weighed one seventy-five when they married, but he must've spent a lot of time working out while they were apart, because moving him felt like trying to push the four-wheeler they'd ridden earlier.

"Isaac. Help me out here."

Wrapping her arms around him, she attempted to lift him enough to get him out of the tub. He pushed off the side with one shoe, flinging himself over with a grunt. Water droplets sprayed her skin like tiny cold bullets. Everly yelped as they landed in a pile of limbs on the slippery floor. She scooted out from under him, one palm set on his chest to keep him upright.

"What happened?"

His eyes glassed over, then finally connected to hers. "That man…jumped me. Office."

"Who, Abbot?"

He shook his head. "Body…guard…"

"James? The big guy?" Oh, no. Isaac was physically fit and average height, around six foot. But the man who'd worked with Hugh looked like one of the professional wrestlers on TV.

"Almost had…him. Someone else came… injected me with something." He arched his shoulder.

"What did they put in you?"

"Not sure," he huffed. "Got the needle…out… woke up in there. Does Lars have…clothes?" He motioned toward the second floor, but his arm flopped back to the tile.

"I'm sure he does. Can you get up? Sit over there, where it's dry? I'll grab something for you to wear." She pointed at the doorway to the hall then gathered him in an awkward side embrace. They hobbled over, exiting the bathroom, and he slid down the wall, his features cramped with discomfort.

He gestured up again. "Hurry. Need to get out of here ASAP."

"How are you going to walk back to Eichhorns?"

"You can carry me." His quicksilver grin, at such close range and shrouded in the intimacy of the shadowy space, kindled a flurry of warmth much too close to her heart.

"I'll do my best."

"You always do."

Everly pondered Isaac's comment as she bounded up the stairs, phone in hand, back into Lars and Ingrid's bedroom. She padded over the thick carpet to the closet. Using her phone light, she eyed the clothes. Two shirts lay on the floor, knocked there earlier when she'd been hiding. Lars had been tall and slim to Isaac's medium, sturdier build, so she rifled through until she found a pair of sweats and a long-sleeved shirt that looked like a close fit. A few coats hung in the corner, and she picked the largest for Isaac and one for her, as well.

Two socks and a dark pair of boots in hand, she dashed out of the closet.

A shimmer of color caught her eye from the nightstand. She trotted over, the wad of clothing tucked beneath one of her arms, the flashlight aimed at the top of a…notebook? The red cover swirled with a silver snowflake pattern, the current year emblazoned with bold gold lettering across the front. Ingrid's daily planner?

"Everly!"

She grabbed the planner and rushed down the stairs. She found him at the end of the hall, propped up in the office doorway.

"Give me the clothes. I think they're back."

TWELVE

Isaac crammed himself through the half-open office window after Everly, then rolled onto the packed snow. Frigid air blasted him, creeping under Lars's coat that Everly had brought down, along with Lars's clothes and boots he'd pulled on.

He grunted at the impact, then stumbled to his feet. Wearing a dead man's clothes sent a shudder through him that had nothing to do with the cold. He shut the window, then tugged Everly's arm as men's voices carried around the building, making the fifteen-yard dash feel like fifty. His weapon was still in its holster, but it'd gotten soaked in the tub, and its usefulness in protecting them was questionable at best.

Isaac struggled to keep up as they bolted into the night. Whatever medication they'd injected him with made everything blurry. A sedative maybe. His head throbbed like a two-day migraine had taken up residence in his skull and refused to move out. Thankfully, he'd fought back enough to knock the needle out before the full amount of medication had been forced into his system. And Everly had been there to save him, hidden on the second floor like a guardian in snow gear.

Speaking of snow... It was piled higher near the metal gate, the hard, crusty surface slick and dangerous. Lars's boots were dead weights attached to his legs as he and Everly bumped along the fence line, searching for the loose panel.

"This is it!" she cried.

They yanked the panel in unison. Pain shimmied up his arm from the wet, reopened barbed-wire wound, and sweat marked his brow despite the numbing temps. A jolt of discomfort twisted across his forehead. He bent in half, banging his shoulder into the metal gate.

"Isaac! Are you okay?"

He fumbled upright, squinting against the ache in his head. "Never...better." He mimicked her words from earlier.

"Are you sure you can do this?"

"Have to." He waved her through the split in the fence, then slipped through after her. "Get to...shed."

Gathering momentum, he followed close behind her, his strides hitching with each heartbeat, pulsing pain through his head. A few feet shy of the small building, a knife of agony slit behind his eyes, and he doubled over.

"Isaac! I hear them!"

The world spun, black dots skimming his vision. *No.* He had to keep her safe. Keep her away from Hugh. Were the men outside the townhouse now? He rolled sideways to counteract his lurching stomach, a groan working up his throat as he retched.

Don't. Stop. Had to…move. He crawled for cover as the world rocked around him, fisting mouthfuls of snow to ease the queasiness. Somewhere behind them, a window scraped open, the sound burning his ears. Were they out of sight yet?

Everly dropped beside him, ramming her shoulder into his backside to propel him the rest of the way into the bushes surrounding the storage shed.

"They just opened the back windows."

"Heard that," he said, grinding out the words.

"Isaac. We need to get you to a doctor."

"Neh. This is just my usual…m-migraine routine." Isaac pushed to a sitting position to check their surroundings. No good. Dizziness washed over him. At least they were well hidden at the moment.

A thought nagged. *The picture.* He'd forgotten it in his wet coat, but what he'd discovered would be enough help. "I found a picture with Lars, Ingrid and Hugh. Hugh used to go by the name Bobby."

He just prayed his phone would come back to life after a dunk in a bowl of rice.

She rubbed her gloved hands over her arms. "Hugh probably wanted the men working for him to call him Bobby, to keep his real identity hidden."

"Right." He rested the heel of his hand on his forehead. "Everything we have on them is circumstantial. We just need to connect the dots with decent evidence." Which was proving harder than he expected. Everly was being sabotaged, along with her dad. But why? What would make Hugh go to these lengths? A thought struck like lightning, and he stumbled upright on wobbly legs. "Your dad wasn't on board with reservations at first, right?"

She rose, wearing a confused expression. "Um, reservations?"

"I mean *renovations*. Brain isn't working." Just what he needed. The remnants of his concussion plus whatever they'd stuck him with made his mind mush.

"My dad wanted basic upgrades. Not a total overhaul of the resort. Hugh's plans required too much money and time and not enough return on investment. He almost let Hugh go a couple months after he hired him." She bulldozed the tip of her boot through the snow. "It was around Hannah's second birthday. I was so busy, and he needed more help."

Isaac tossed out a harsh breath. If only he'd been here, maybe Hugh wouldn't have been hired in the first place. Maybe he could've proved himself to Ted Raven.

"I'm sorry." The simple words carried little weight unless he helped her *now*.

"I know you are."

"Your dad was right."

"About what?" she demanded. "Did something happen between you and my dad in the hospital in France?"

Along with warning him to stay out of Everly's life, Ted Raven had told him to keep quiet about getting Isaac's mom's record cleared. "It's nothing."

"It must be something."

"He reminded me that I didn't fit in at Raven's." Isaac rubbed his fingertips into his temples. "Said you could do better, and that I wasn't welcome here. My accident confirmed it. I flew across the world trying to better myself when I should've just stayed here, with you."

"That's why you acted so angry and distant?

Because of your accident and because my dad said those awful things?"

"Partly, yes. The concussion caused bad migraines, and the painkillers the doctors gave me messed with my mind. Plus, I was mad about everything." He stared at the townhouse to keep from making eye contact. "I was upset with myself for taking that risk. It was proof."

"Proof of what? That you were a young guy who made a mistake?" Tears threaded her voice.

His muscles twitched from remaining dizziness and from the urge to hold her. To protect her, forever. But he'd given up that right when he left. He cleared his throat. "Proof that I wasn't good enough for you."

There. The words were out. Finally, the truth.

"So…" Her wary pause pushed the air from his lungs. "You asked for a divorce because my dad butted into our marriage, and because you felt like you weren't good enough for me?"

The truth was surprisingly easy to admit despite the burden of years he'd buried it under. "That about covers it. Oh, and the quote your dad gave to the *Sun-Times* about my accident, painting me as the villain in the incident."

Isaac Rhodes is a reckless American journalist who doesn't represent Raven's Fun Runs. He endangered himself and others and nearly took the life of French skier Marcus Beauvoir.

"Yes. That. I saw what he told the French reporter, and I'm sorry. I knew Marcus challenged you that morning, and he wasn't even that close to you when you crashed. But Isaac…"

He waited, and it felt like his entire life lead up to this point.

"I wish you would've told me back then."

"Yeah, well, I kind of wish I had too."

"I didn't care about any of that stuff."

But I did.

A car's engine broke the trance, and they ducked, waiting. They were on the backside of the townhouses, and the parking lot lay in the front, so he had to determine what was happening by sound instead of sight. Probing twin headlights appeared on the road, splitting the dark as a vehicle drove away from Lars's house, following Fall Line Road. The noise from its engine slowly died off as night swallowed the headlights.

"They're leaving?" Everly asked.

"Sounds like it." For now. Isaac set the heel of one hand to his forehead to relieve the pressure from his headache. They must've used some kind of surgical sedative.

Everly clasped his arm. "Can you run?"

"I'm going to try."

They set off in a crouching jog across the fields. Packed Powder Putt-Putt's gate interrupted their trajectory, and by silent agreement they skirted the mini-golf area. It would take longer, but Isaac wasn't sure he had it in him to climb fences at the moment. Twice he had to slow down as lightning bolts sliced across his skull. Everly hovered over him until the pain diminished and he found his footing in the snow.

Eichhorns sat as silent as a tomb, the windows dark and curtains drawn. The parking lot stretched out, empty.

"Looks quiet."

"Sheila won't be up for a few more hours." Everly motioned at the restaurant. "Let's get you inside."

They edged the perimeter of the parking lot, moving toward the back of the restaurant. At the door, Everly tugged on his arm.

"Let me go in first, in case Alpine forgets you're one of the good guys."

She was right. The dog wouldn't let an intruder in, and he was still new to Alpine. Better to be cautious. Everly slipped past and disappeared inside. The click of canine nails and Everly's soft murmuring let him know all was well. He entered next, whispering Alpine's name. In the dark room, a cold nose bumped his hand, and her thick tail thumped against his leg.

She leaned her weight into him for attention. "Alpine. Hey, girl." He scratched her neck and back. Everly rose from her crouch, tying her arms in a knot across her middle.

"What do we do now?"

"Get my phone in rice." Isaac shrugged Lars's coat off and pointed at the pantry, raising his hands in a silent question.

Everly tiptoed to the bifold door, flipped on a small light, then disappeared inside. A few seconds later she reappeared, a box in hand. She located a glass mixing bowl in a bottom cupboard, opened the rice and poured it in, then waved him over. He pulled out his phone, hitting the power button again. The black screen only reflected the stark outline of his face in the crackled glass.

He buried the phone, then turned, pointing toward the stairs. "I'll give it an hour or so in the rice. Why don't you go upstairs?"

"What if you can't get the pictures off of it?"

"I'm more concerned with contacting Dan. He needs to know what happened."

She offered him her cell. "You can use mine."

"Too risky." He shook his head. "I just wish I'd found something concrete at Lars's."

Her eyes rounded, then she unzipped her jacket and tugged out a shiny notebook. "I grabbed this upstairs, in Lars and Ingrid's bedroom."

"Huh. Ingrid's?"

"I think so."

He eyed the feminine cover then leafed through it. The calendar was marked up already, names and notes scribbled throughout. She was a busy woman, that much was clear.

It was doubtful the planner offered any pertinent information, but he'd learned never to dismiss any part of an investigation. Even the most trivial. He motioned at the stairs. "You head up while I take a look. Try to rest. Please."

Her lovely features gathered in a fatigued frown as she inched toward the stairwell. "What about you?"

"I'll sleep when this is over." He couldn't consider sleep with the men still after them and the connection to Hugh Markham dangling like a severed power line. Not to mention Everly as a person of interest in the case and their daughter's safety holding his thoughts hostage.

She ascended two steps, Alpine at her heels, then turned and met his eyes. Quiet memories wavered between them, the good and bad. All of it. "Thank you for telling me what really happened."

"I'd say it was about time."

Her frown smoothed out. "Past time."

"Yeah. And thanks for saving me back there."

Her lips curved upward, the smile starting

small and growing until his chest ached. "I guess we're even now."

"Everly." A male voice tugged her from the fog of sleep. "Wake up."

She pushed upright, squinting around the room. Sunlight spilled through the windows, creating long fingers of yellow light that stretched across the floor.

Where—?

Eichhorns. With Isaac. Lars's murder and all the details came crashing back. *Person of interest.* She clutched the blanket like it was a shield against all the bad memories of the last two days. "Isaac? What happened? Your phone—?"

"It's working again. I contacted Dan." His words rushed out, bumping into each other, and his gaze skipped around the room. Avoiding hers.

"What is it? What's wrong?"

"I went to the kitchen to grab some coffee and…" An odd mix of emotions played over his face. "Becca and Hannah are downstairs." He strode out of the room, shutting the door.

Leaving her wide-eyed and heart heavy. *Hannah.*

Everly jumped out of bed, caught her hair into a ponytail and pulled on clean clothes, then hurried out into the hallway. She found Isaac standing in front of a picture in the hallway, his hands balled up at his sides. *Oh.* It was taken at Packed Powder Putt-Putt with her and her dad, Hannah, and Sheila. It'd been a relaxed and memorable June evening—Everly's birthday celebration. Hannah was about two, her dimpled smile and thick brown hair tamed into two crooked pigtails.

His fists opened, fingers spreading wide as though searching for something solid to grasp. "Was it your birthday?"

"Yes."

"Hannah is…she's beautiful like her mom."

She flushed at the compliment. "I can't wait for you to meet her." She gave his hand a squeeze, and he captured hers inside his own. Isaac's steady warmth seeped into her palm, more effective than caffeine. This connection between them originated from their mutual love of their daughter. That was it.

He pulled away. "I can't stand this."

Did he mean about Hannah, or them? Or *both*?

She drew in a steadying breath. *Get it together, Everly.* "There's a spot in the kitchen where we can look out and not be seen. But we'd have to be very quiet. Hannah will make a racket if she sees me." Her throat constricted. She missed those sturdy little arms and her daughter's sweet strawberry smell, the way her thick hair—so like Isaac's—tickled Everly's nose when Hannah hugged her.

They descended the stairs quietly, and Everly strained to catch any noises from below. The hallway between the kitchen and restaurant sounded clear at the moment. She took the last step and ducked behind the cabinets along the wall, Isaac shadowing her as they inched toward the customer bathroom.

It was a risk. If Becca or Hannah had to use the restroom, she and Isaac would be forced to dart back down the hall and up the stairs.

"They're here early." He nodded at the hallway clock, which indicated it was five minutes before 7:00 a.m.

"Hannah's a morning person like someone else I know." She tapped her elbow to his ribs.

"Ah, sorry about that."

"She's worth it."

The double swinging doors were flanked by bar openings on either side, like open windows. During season, Sheila would set the full plates on the counter so Trixie and Barb could deliver them to hungry patrons. But both women had been sent home after Lars's murder.

She and Isaac crawled to the open section and rose inch by inch until they peeked over. Across the dining room, Becca sat at a booth with her back to them. She leaned to her left side and tilted her head like she was listening to a sound coming from the wall. A familiar head popped up beside her, a smile tipping Hannah's rosebud mouth.

He let out a hushed exhale. "She's…amazing."

"She is."

"And she's actually mine."

"Yes—ours."

Becca reached over with a hungry hand monster aimed for their ticklish daughter's side, and Hannah's high-pitched giggles exploded into the reverent silence.

"How's it possible I love her when I haven't met her yet?"

Yet.

Her hand brushed his, giving it a squeeze. Then she turned it palm-up. Habit? She wasn't sure. But when he covered it and threaded their fingers, his bright gaze aimed at their daughter, an old wound in her heart sealed up. Restored.

She caught a shimmer on his face. He swiped at the tear with his other hand. Sheila carried a tray toward Becca and Hannah, a glass of orange juice and a juice box atop it. The older woman set them down and engaged Hannah in a lively conversation.

Becca nodded at whatever Sheila said, then turned her head.

Her friend's stormy blue eyes landed on Everly, then flicked to Isaac seconds before he ducked. Everly did the same, her free hand fisted over her mouth. "Becca saw me."

"She saw both of us."

Everly couldn't help it. She drew up to her knees to get another glimpse.

Becca was facing forward again, drawing something for Hannah, probably on a napkin. The jingling bells on the restaurant's front door sounded.

Hugh Markham strode into Eichhorns, flanked by the two men who'd gone after them on Tipping Point. Abbot and Eddy.

THIRTEEN

Sheila called out a hello, then turned toward the kitchen, her brows drawn tight, before facing Hugh again. Everly shrank into a ball next to Isaac.

Did Sheila know Everly and Isaac were downstairs?

"Good morning, gentlemen. You ready for some sausage and egg casserole? It's got a nice kick to it, the way you like it, Hugh."

"Ted Raven prefers the spicy dishes." The irritation in his voice set Everly's nerves on edge. "Not me. It would be nice if you got that straight for once."

One of the men with him chuckled.

"Oh, sure. That's right. And how is Teddy doing? Have you heard anything?" she prodded.

"Sounds like he pulled through okay. This time."

Everly puffed her cheeks with air to keep

from spewing off at the mouth. How dare Hugh act like this when he'd *caused* her dad's illness?

"That's something to be thankful for."

Hugh grunted but kept his thoughts to himself for once.

"I'm so glad Teddy's okay," Sheila chattered on, the clatter of silverware punctuating her words. "We can't bear any more bad news at Raven's. As far as the casserole, I can sprinkle on more cheese and add butter if that will—"

"Just dish it up and get it out here. I'm starving. Three plates. Three cups of coffee."

"You got it." Sheila scurried through the swinging doors, right past them.

In the dining room, Hugh let out a low whistle. "Well, look who's here. Isn't this Ms. Raven's daughter?"

Becca murmured an affirmative answer but said nothing else to Hugh's prying.

"And what's the little girl's name? Heather?" Hugh asked.

Isaac's chest expanded, the cords of his forearm muscle bunching against Everly. She gripped his wrist. They couldn't move now or they'd be discovered.

"No, it's Hannah."

Which Hugh already knew. Was he trying to fluster Becca? Her poor friend.

"Ah, that's right. *Hannah*." A wave of nausea rolled over Everly at the way Hugh said their daughter's name. "What're you two having for breakfast? The sausage casserole Sheila mentioned?"

"No, bagels with cream cheese and OJ." Becca's impatient tone told Everly her friend wasn't buying into his blathering friendliness.

"Seems awful cold to be venturing out for food you could make at home."

Everly ground her back teeth together. He was testing Becca. Seeing if any information slipped about her and Isaac's whereabouts.

"Hannah and I are going to make cookies with Sheila."

"Two days after a man's murdered on-site, and you're making cookies."

Everly's hand clenched Isaac's, picturing Hugh's grim smile and thinning, oily hair as he hovered over Becca and Hannah, a vulturous look on his face.

"I needa go potty."

Hannah's sweet voice.

Isaac yanked free. *Move*, his eyes warned.

They scrambled down the hall like human crabs, silence the highest goal. Hannah's prancing steps through the dining room covered the sounds of their escape.

Jabbing his thumb at a narrow broom closet beside the women's bathroom, Isaac opened the creaky door and thrust Everly inside, then followed.

Soft material scraped her face. Jackets? A plastic vacuum or sweeper handle leaned against the wall, then fell into her leg. He stopped the door just short of slamming and latched it so quietly Everly didn't hear the click with the coats crammed around her head. Dust tickled her nose.

Had Hugh and his men heard them?

Isaac backed up until he bumped the coats. "You okay?"

He meant well, but acknowledging her claustrophobia just made it more pronounced. Loud steps and lighter, irregular steps sounded from outside the closet. "Wonderful."

"Focus on Hannah." He turned his head and pressed his mouth to her hair. "She's so close."

"If she saw me now, she'd be really loud." How would Hannah react to Isaac? She was hesitant around strangers, but once she warmed up, she became an adorable, curious shadow.

The steady rise and fall of Isaac's chest calmed Everly. Just like he always had.

Through the thin walls, they could hear a toilet flushed, then the faucet turned on. Voices mingled, interspersed with giggles. Hannah was almost done. Becca's voice caught Everly, and she touched her ear to the wall as yearning gained a chokehold on her emotions. When would she hold her daughter again?

"Mommy misses you, Bunny. You'll see her soon."

"Pwease can we see her now?"

Becca murmured back. The bathroom door creaked open, and Hannah's dancing steps ran ahead of Becca's. Everly reached up, her hand brushing the doorknob, her arms so empty. A sob wedged in her chest as Hannah headed back to the dining room area.

Another set of footsteps neared, heavier and clipped. *Hugh?*

"Where is your friend?"

"I have lots of friends," Becca shot back. "I don't keep tabs on them all."

"Enough with the games. Where is Ms. Raven?"

Isaac clenched his fists as Hugh questioned Becca. He fought to keep his uneven breaths from blasting into the musty coats barely shielding their presence in the closet. The resort manager's fake friendliness from the dining room had fled, leaving behind a steel-edged determination that prickled the hairs on Isaac's arms. What was the man after?

"I asked you a question."

"I'm *not sure* where she is. Somewhere in Maple Creek is all I know."

Laughter exploded from Hugh like a spray of bullets. "Why do I not believe that?"

Isaac eased his weight from one foot to the other, only his FBI training holding him still.

Hugh continued. "You best keep in mind aiding and abetting criminals carries its own sentence. That cute little girl out there? She'll be shoved into foster care when all three of you are behind bars—including her deadbeat dad."

Isaac gritted his teeth until pain shot up his neck.

Everly's warm fingertips found and cradled his jaw as though she understood the war his body waged to keep quiet after Hugh's insolence.

"My friend didn't kill Lars. And you know it."

"Oh, but I think she did. Evidence is stacking up, young lady. She found the body. The bloody shirt in her office. And her running confirms her guilt."

"Her running confirms she's being chased."

"Chased? Now where did you get *that* idea from?" His sneer was a knife scraping one of Sheila's dinner plates. "Sounds like someone called you."

"Are we done? I'd like to finish my breakfast."

A shuffling and shadows connecting underneath the bottom of the door betrayed Hugh inching closer to Becca. "I have eyes all over this resort. Mark my words. They will be caught."

Becca took off down the hall. Sheila's hesitant steps approached as though she were walking through a minefield.

"Everything all right, Hugh? Your food's up."

"About time." He pivoted and strode away.

Isaac sagged against the side of the closet. Everly attempted to drop her hand, but he recaptured it.

"Your breathing okay?"

"I wanted to throttle that man so much I forgot I hate tight spaces."

"That makes two of us who want to throttle him." He squeezed her hand, then released it. "Justice is coming Hugh's way. And I'll be the one serving it."

"But what if we can't find enough evidence?"

Isaac squared his shoulders, and an empty hanger bumped his back. "Dan's getting me the go-ahead to check one more location. He pulled a warrant and should hear back from the judge any minute. He's also been in touch with the Maple Creek PD. They're aware the FBI is in the area for this investigation. They've given you till four o'clock today to turn yourself in."

"Turn myself in." She spoke in a robotic voice.

"To answer more questions." *Please, God, let that be all.*

He couldn't have another woman he loved spend time behind bars. "But first we need to get out of this closet. I'm going to choke to death on the smell of mothballs and feet and sweaty ski gear."

She muffled a snicker. "You too? I love you, but I do not want to be stuck in another closet with you ever again. No offense."

Everly turned into a statue beside him, and his tongue dried up like a lump of cotton as her words echoed in the small space. *I love you.*

Sweat prickled her scalp. Had she really just said that?

"That didn't…" *Come out like I planned.* Heat flooded her cheeks, and the air in the small space charged with awareness. "I mean, I did—"

He chuckled, but the strained sound vanished in the crammed closet. "No worries."

"It just…slipped out."

"Everly, drop it." He edged closer to the door.

She clenched her eyes shut as a kaleidoscope of regret swirled behind her eyelids. Why did it have to be so complicated between them?

"During my training I learned that people in high-stress situations like ours revert to sharing random facts and revealing strange thoughts and feelings they don't really mean. Others spill the truth since everything else is stripped away, but most likely you're reverting back to…before."

Others spill the truth since everything else is stripped away.

He cleared his throat. "Can you count off ten minutes? To keep you distracted?"

Ten more minutes in this closet? "I'll try."

Nine and a half minutes later, with only Sheila's footsteps traipsing up and down the hall periodically, Isaac inched forward. "I'm going to check."

She drew to her feet as the door creaked, light piercing the narrow opening. Her breath whooshed in and out. *Fresh air.*

Sheila's face appeared. "*In the closet?* I thought you two had gone back upstairs. I can't deal with this." She rested her head on the door frame, squashing the dark hair threaded with gray. "I was a mess out there. They're gone. Asked for to-go boxes and stormed out."

"I'm so sorry." Everly slipped the rest of the way out of the closet. "What about Becca…?" *And Hannah.*

"They left, too, doll. I'm sorry. Becca got upset

with Hugh and all his pestering, I think. She said she'd rather make cookies another time."

Everly blinked back the crushing disappointment. She knew it was better for her roommate and Hannah to stay at their apartment. But that couldn't stop her longing to feel her daughter's little face nestled in the crook of her neck.

Isaac turned to Sheila. "We need your help."

"Anything for you two."

"Hugh and his men aren't allowed in the kitchen. They don't make coffee for anyone and they don't touch the food."

Sheila snapped her back straight like he'd announced Eichhorns was going low-carb. "I would never pass off my duties to a man like that. This is *my* kitchen."

"It's not you we're worried about, it's—"

"We believe Hugh's been poisoning my dad."

Sheila slapped a hand over her mouth before sputtering out a reply. "Oh, poor Teddy. You mean to tell me Hugh did it on purpose?"

"We don't have time to go into more detail." Isaac shook his head at Everly, then addressed Sheila. "Please keep the kitchen clear. Now, did Hugh say where he was going?"

"Well, I did overhear him mention meeting a local detective in town later."

She and Isaac exchanged a loaded look. His

phone chirped, and he slipped it out, mouth scrunching up at whatever text came over the screen.

"Okay." He tucked his cell back in his pocket and met Everly's questioning gaze. "Do you have access to a vehicle?"

"You're welcome to use my van, doll. Keys are hanging by the back door."

Isaac surprised Everly by wrapping Sheila in a quick hug. "You're the best." The older woman hummed with delight at the warm gesture. He pulled away and motioned Everly toward the kitchen. She strode after Isaac, his affectionate behavior and Sheila's information about Hugh buzzing around in her head like a lost bumblebee.

"Did you tell Dan about Detective Savage?"

He snagged a jacket off the coatrack, tossed it her way, then slipped on a larger one. "Yes. Dan checked out Savage. If the man's involved with Hugh, he kept his hands clean."

Everly worried her lower lip with her teeth. The day of Lars's murder, the detective's questions had seemed pointed and invasive, his gaze penetrating as he interviewed her. Maybe that was standard police procedure? She certainly didn't have any experience being interviewed by officers.

After grabbing a bagel from the counter and two water bottles, she followed Isaac out the back door. Chickadees and blue jays flitted around Sheila's bird feeder, searching the snow for seeds. The day was bright and unnervingly quiet, the fresh snow glistening under a blue sky. It was unsettling to see the resort devoid of traffic on the slopes and on the road.

"Where are we going?"

"To Hugh's. Dan just confirmed a callback from the judge. Search warrant is good to go. Since Dan's in town and I'm closer, I'm heading over."

Hugh's? Fear pushed her rib cage into her spine. "What if he comes back from the meeting early?"

Isaac's mouth compressed. "Let's pray he doesn't."

Isaac studied the white van as Everly peeled off the Eichhorns Meats and Eats magnet from its side. The vehicle's tinted windows would provide a semblance of cover on their way across the resort. While he hesitated to bring Everly along, she was safest at his side.

Two questions plagued him: How long would Hugh be in town meeting with Detective Savage, and were the two men working together?

When Dan texted him inside the restaurant, he informed Isaac about a call scheduled with a former committee member from the US Ski and Snowboard Association. A promising lead, Dan said. The possible witness had served with Hugh on the finance committee and worked with him in Park City. The man said he had information about Hugh's questionable financial practices. When the witness heard about the murder at Raven's, he got in touch with the local authorities in Utah, who'd contacted Dan. Still, would it be enough to charge Hugh with a crime?

Everly set the magnetic signs aside and stepped next to him. "You don't think the police checked Hugh's townhouse?"

"They did an initial sweep per protocol. I'm looking for something specific."

"Poison."

"Yes."

"How are you feeling? Your arm—I see the way you're holding it." She imitated the careful movement.

"I'm fine. I rewrapped it while you were sleeping. Do you mind driving? You know the resort better, and that way I can keep an eye on our surroundings."

Four minutes later Everly steered them out to

Fall Line Road. The landscape spread out like a white carpet, the flat valley rising to meet the empty slopes and eerily still lifts. Trees lined the mountainsides in between the slopes, snow-capped and silent.

"Oh." Everly tipped her head back. "I grabbed the planner I found last night. It's in the bag." She motioned to the backpack-style purse she'd borrowed from Sheila. It lay rumpled on the seat behind him.

"I flipped through it last night but didn't notice anything out of the ordinary. There's Lars's place." Isaac motioned to the townhouse community surrounded by a tall black gate. The scene of last night's altercation. "They've updated those, haven't they? They look different now that I can see them in the daylight."

"Yeah, they've been updated," she whispered, but her eyes lit on him, not the buildings. "A lot has changed around here. You've changed too, Isaac."

Was it his imagination, or had her voice softened on that last sentence? "Guess I have."

"Sheila's so happy to see you back here, you know."

He shrugged, pushing down the onslaught of emotions her words brought on. "Feels more like I let her down. Disappointed another person who cared for me."

"She doesn't hold grudges." Everly's fingers skimmed the steering wheel. "How is it, being back?"

As much as he tried to treat this case like any other, reality was that it wasn't. His heart was just as involved as his head. "Other than the investigation and your case?"

She released a hard breath. "Other than that."

He gazed through the windshield, taking in the scenic landscape, the rise and fall of the stunning land her family had owned for generations. "I've been across the ocean, visited other countries. But no place stayed with me like Raven's."

"Come on, even France?"

"The best scenery was right in front of me the entire time." He stared out the window so she couldn't see his face. "I just wish I'd appreciated it when I had the chance."

She took a right-hand turn toward the far end of the valley but didn't say anything else. Maybe he'd said too much. The buildings thinned out, with more space between structures. A sign for hikers jutted from the roadside, pointing into the woods.

He twisted side to side, stretching his back. "We have to be on the lookout. Hugh might have posted a guard at his place, or near it."

She murmured agreement. "We're here."

Ahead lay a cluster of two-story buildings, slate gray with white shutters, hedged in by a perimeter of well-maintained shrubs decorated with the newest snowfall. A ten-foot gate surrounded the townhouses. Four dozen units, give or take, each two stories, were designed with a modern architecture that clashed with the old-style German-village feel of the rest of the resort. Each unit boasted a wide expanse of windows and a set of double doors linked to the main walkway by a private path. Snow blanketed the sidewalks.

"These look fancy."

"They better be for what it cost to build them." She drove through the empty parking lot, then slowed at the far end.

Isaac pointed to a parking spot on the side of the building. It was hidden from anyone driving through the entrance. She maneuvered the van to the farthest spot and set it in Park beside a single-story gray building that mirrored the townhouses' look but was much smaller.

"What is this?" He motioned at the shed.

"The dumpster's inside here, and there are maintenance supplies too. It's all very aesthetic." She rolled her eyes. "That's the transformer over there, behind that hedge."

"How much is he charging for these places?"

"Too much." She scowled at the structures.

"We're usually fully booked early December through end of February. New Year's weekend we were at seventy percent capacity. Dad was upset. Lars too. And Hugh purchased five new snowmobiles last month, for staff. More like for himself and his assistants. They have quieter engines so as *not to distract the patrons*." Sarcasm dripped off her words.

"Why did your dad hand over so much control to Hugh?"

One of her shoulders rose. "Hugh wanted the control, and with dad's health…" She unbuckled her seatbelt. "With it deteriorating, he didn't have a lot of choice about letting Hugh take charge. Hugh was relentless about overhauling Raven's."

"Lars never wanted in on it? Part-ownership or anything?"

"Lars loves—loved—to ski. His sole passion was teaching others to love it, too. He liked to have a say in things here, but I don't think he ever wanted to run this place."

"There's something to be said for that," Isaac noted quietly. "At least he died doing what he loved."

She seemed to shrink beside him, and Isaac grimaced. Bad choice of words. "I'm sorry, I shouldn't have brought up…"

She waved it off. "It's okay."

He clamped his jaw and peered around. An army of trees flanked each side of the community, and beyond that, a service road stretched into the mountains. No sounds or movement except the occasional whirl of the wind.

Everly shouldered her backpack, then they exited the vehicle and jogged to the nearest unit. After skirting the edge of the building, Isaac held up a hand and slowed, sweeping the surroundings. "I want to go in the back. In and out. Fast. Clean."

She nodded. "This way."

They continued around the structures until she grabbed his arm, signaling at Hugh's unit. They slunk to the side of the building and made their way toward the back. Each unit offered a double window situated on the first floor, while the wood deck had a covered hot tub and faced the snowcapped mountains in the distance.

"Nice view." He pulled his hat off and shoved it into his coat pocket. Wiping the sweat from his brow, he shot Everly an appraising look. "You up for a climb?"

"As long as it's not in a closet, sure."

His cell phone vibrated in his jacket pocket, and Isaac retrieved it. "Hold up." Dan's name filled the top of the screen. He skimmed the message twice, his pulse kicking into overdrive.

Park City case: Witness admits to helping Hugh Markham filter USSA monies through fake account to open two businesses. Witness asked for immunity for the case in exchange for information. Search warrant for Hugh's Maple Creek townhome and Park City authorities is signed and authorities are reaching out to Hugh immediately. Be on the alert.

Also, you were correct about Ted Raven's diagnosis. His doctor returned my call. Minute traces of ethylene glycol were found in his system. There's liver damage but the doctor thinks he'll pull through.

"Isaac? Is it about my dad?"

He gripped the cell and read the text to her.

She moaned. "I wish I'd recognized this was happening. How could I not have—"

"Don't beat yourself up. Believe me, I've done it for years. Pummeling yourself about the past doesn't accomplish anything but mess you up today. God doesn't want us living like that."

She gazed at him like he was an intricate puzzle she needed to solve. "I'm sorry you did that."

"My behavior was pretty awful to you, Everly."

She stepped away from him, hands clasped. "It's okay, you know. I understand more about what happened and... I forgive you."

"Thank you." He cleared his throat and looked away from her soul-deep stare. "Also, it appears Hugh's sins from Park City are catching up to him."

"That's good, right?"

"Absolutely. It put him on the authorities' radar as a person of interest for this case, and the warrant was just signed."

"Thank You, God." She let out a grateful murmur, then shocked him by leaning close to wrap him in a quick, tight hug. "Thank *you* for coming back. It means the world to me. And to my dad, even though he'll never admit it."

He ducked his chin in a nod, tucking her words away for later. Back to business. "Listen, I want you to stay outside on the deck while I go in. Behind the hot tub so you're not out in the open. Knock on the glass slider if anything unusual happens."

"Okay."

"I'm going to lift you up there first. Ready?"

He threaded his gloves and motioned for her to step on them. She did and set a hand on his shoulder. Isaac lifted her toward the wall and railing. "Grab on and pull yourself up."

Everly squirmed for the deck floor and finally grasped the railing, and he pressed her body up. She twined her arms through, then dragged herself over the top, Sheila's little backpack purse flopping around with the effort.

Her boot dug for the hole in the railing and she clambered over. "Made it." She glanced down at him, then out over the landscape. A strange look crossed her face.

"What's wrong?" He whipped around. Nothing but trees and snow and the backdrop of pure white mountains lay behind them.

"There's a vehicle parked past the service road."

FOURTEEN

Everly's heart rate, already elevated from the climb, took off in a sprint. She gripped the railing and gaped from the unknown vehicle to Isaac, standing at full alert below.

"Is it a resort truck?" Isaac leaped up, grasping the edge of the deck, then levered himself over. He landed with a thud next to her.

"No. Looks like a four-by-four Jeep. I don't recognize it."

He tugged her so they were kneeling, hidden behind the hot tub. "Did you see anyone inside it?"

"No. I don't see anything or anyone." She rose on her knees in order to keep her eyes glued to the navy SUV.

He crawled over to the slider and jimmied the doors until the metal stick holding them together gave way. Every few seconds he glanced back.

She angled her face to get the best view of the vehicle. "Still no sign of anyone."

"Hugh may have set up a dummy car to scare us away." Isaac slid the door open. "If you hear or see anything, any movement from the vehicle, knock on the glass."

"I will."

He slipped through the slider and disappeared into the dark confines of the townhouse, and she crouched on the side of the hot tub. Solitude hit her like a blizzard's blast, and a shiver of unease crept over her limbs. *Please, God, keep him safe. Keep us both safe.*

She stuck her head out from behind the hot tub just enough to keep an eye on the vehicle. No sound came from the area except the occasional moan of the wind and a creaking noise on a neighbor's deck. The unit heaters were turned down, so the inside temps would be cold. She edged toward the slider, feeling the air drifting out. Warm. Which meant Hugh had been here recently.

Everly shuddered. What could she do while she waited? The backpack burned a trail over her shoulder. The planner. She unzipped the bag, retrieved the small book and began leafing through the pages. Nothing stood out as unusual. A note on a date here, a star marking another date there. Ingrid's bold cursive matched her strong personality.

Everly lifted her face, tracing the landscape,

mashing her mouth into a frown at the sight of the immobile vehicle. Whose was it, and why was it parked there?

She dropped her gaze to the planner, flipping through from March to January and back. Then she scanned the last month, December. Another month was tacked on, this one January of the next year. Everly narrowed her eyes at a note Ingrid had penciled in for next January.

Ingrid had drawn a star on the weekend of the US Alpine Challenge and beside that written one word. *Hosting.* But that was impossible—

A car door shut, and she gripped the planner to her chest. That sound had been muffled on purpose. Her muscles constricted. Slowly, Everly poked her head out again. Nothing but pristine winter landscape, the plaintive howl of the wind, and the lonely cry of a raven somewhere in the woods. She loosened her death grip on the planner and glanced at the sliding door. Where was Isaac? It'd been at least three minutes since he went inside.

Should she knock on the glass, even though she didn't see anyone?

"He's inside, but where's the girl?"

Everly barely caught her scream in time. She lunged at the slider and rapped her knuckles so hard on the glass that pain shot up her arm.

"What was that?"

The men's voices carried up from the side of the unit, their footsteps silent in the snow. As soon as she stood, they'd see her. Indecision warred, and Hannah's sweet face filled her frantic vision. Jump down and run, leaving Isaac behind, or stay hidden?

"They went in the deck!"

Too late. Everly's heart crashed into her ribs as the men approached the back of the unit cautiously, their voices frighteningly familiar. James? She readied her body for a leap off the railing, but could she outrun them?

"Maybe he went inside?"

"Course he did, that's why they're here. Boss said to get the girl and eliminate the man."

Eliminate the man. Everly bit her cheek as a sob formed in her throat.

"He's federal."

The man threw out an oath. "I'm just following orders."

Before she had time to react, the deck wiggled and a man grunted. Close. So close. One of them was climbing onto the deck.

"I'll go to the front and make sure he doesn't get out that way." Footsteps took the other man away, leaving Everly with only one. But should she warn Isaac again, or take off? She knew

Isaac would want her gone. Safe. Far from these men. But she couldn't leave him.

She held her breath as the man grunted again and squirmed his way onto the deck. She hid behind the hot tub, her bag in hand. It was all she had for a weapon. That and surprise.

The man's shoes slapped the deck, and blood swirled in her ears. Now was her chance—

Everly sprang to her feet, the bag swinging out, directly into the man's surprised face. He shoved one arm out to block it, but not before the backpack smacked his face and neck. Before he could react, she rushed him, ramming a shoulder into his chest. But she'd overcompensated, and with nothing to hold on to, she fell forward as the man fell back against the deck rail. He hit it hard, growling in pain, and one of his arms snaked out to wrap around her.

She screamed, trying to draw a knee up to score his groin. He twisted away just in time, and seconds later Everly found herself face-to-face with the man's small black gun.

James sneered at her, his arm a thick rope around her neck. "You and that man of yours are a handful. But you're not getting away this time. This time, Boss gets what he wants."

"No!" She fought with her back and legs as he withdrew a tan rag from his coat pocket.

None of her effort dislodged her from his shackling grip.

"This part won't hurt a bit, sweetheart. Just breathe."

She shrieked into his palm as he brought the rag to her mouth. A noxious smell filled her nose, coating her tongue. *Please, God, no.* Her muscles twitched, and she held her breath.

But she couldn't hold it forever. When her chest was on fire, lungs crying out for reprieve, she sucked in a desperate gulp of oxygen. Everything blurred, and her muscles slackened.

She felt herself being dragged toward the sliding doors.

He yanked off one of her gloves and pressed her hand to the glass and then doorjamb. "A few fingerprints here, a few fingerprints there. And now we say bye to this fella. Incoming!" In slow motion, James's free arm flung something small and black inside the upstairs room. *Isaac.*

Then darkness swallowed her whole.

Isaac coughed hard, his whole frame shaking as he cleared the smoldering air from his lungs. He grimaced, squinting at his surroundings.

Smoke tinged the air, and decimated furniture lay in rubble around him. He inched away from the broken glass and wood, leaving behind a trail of blood. From the feel of it, his arm wound reopened—and who knew what else? A rip in his coat let in cold air that bit at his exposed skin.

Had Hugh's men tossed a bomb inside?

Everly. Did she get away? *Please, God, protect her.*

He turned over, feeling for his cell phone. Empty pockets. It must've been dislodged when the bomb went off. Thankfully he hadn't been near the sliding glass doors upstairs when it detonated.

Isaac struggled upright, his throat on fire. He eyed the immediate area for his phone. No sign of it, just mangled debris everywhere. A hole rimmed with red and black made a messy circle on the ceiling. Only a chemical-laden explosive could cause that kind of damage. He'd been tussling with one of the men when a voice above and outside shouted a warning, and the man fighting him tried to get away. But then the blast had sent them both flying and must've opened up the gaping hole above his head.

He clambered to his feet, his leg muscles shaky and chest tight. Where was the—

Across the room, a hefty dresser covered the torso, upper body and head of the perp he'd been wrestling with—Abbot, by the height of the man. Isaac grimaced. It must've fallen through with the explosion. Abbot's motionless legs and the weight of the furniture that landed on him likely meant the bomb had caused a fatality—just not the one the men had intended.

Thank You, God, for protecting me. Please protect Everly until I get there.

He felt for his weapon. At least his gun was still intact, if not his cell. While Dan would tell him to wait for backup, all he could see was Everly's face outside as she hugged him. The gratitude and hope in her eyes. He had to find her.

Isaac stumbled down the hallway, shoving aside an upended recliner as he made his way to the front door. It swung open from the blast, hanging from the hinges. He canvased the area, then jogged to Sheila's van, packed snow crunching underfoot. The vehicle's front tires sat lower than the back, slashed. His frustrated groan caught on the wind. The men must've gotten to it before entering Hugh's unit.

In the driver's window, his embattled, desperate reflection frowned back. What could he do now? No cell phone, no vehicle. His gentle admonition to Everly outside the cabin on Tipping Point Mountain returned to him, God's word living and active. *Walk by faith, not by sight.*

"Lord, please help me find Everly. Keep her safe until I do. Guide my steps. I don't know where she is."

Something nagged him, calling him back inside. Isaac left the van, returning to the spot in Hugh's place where he'd woken up after the bomb detonated. He peered around, eyes pinpointing any object that looked like his cell or—

Skis! Set on the wall as decoration. He crossed the messy room, avoiding razor-sharp shards of glass from the coffee table and broken picture frames. Now was as good a time as any to put the equipment to use. Losing contact with Dan wasn't ideal, but his instincts and his knowledge of this resort would have to be enough of a guide.

After hefting the skis off the rack, Isaac ran his palm along the base of them, then snatched up the poles. Cross-country skis. He hadn't skied since his accident, and the memory of those painful days rose like a dark cloud over him.

He paired them together and turned, shaking away the unwelcome recollection. *Focus*. Cross-country skis needed special boots. Had Hugh kept his inside? Isaac's gaze landed on a closet door beside the front door. He rushed over and ripped it open. Coats, goggles and shoes atop boxes… *There*. A pair of expensive ski boots, tags still attached. He ripped the tags off, snagged some goggles and burst back outside, worry for Everly driving every movement and breath.

She needed him.

Isaac slowed, the gear swinging from his grasp. Everly was grateful for his help, glad he'd get to know his daughter, but he was fooling himself if he thought she still needed him for anything other than this investigation. Not after the way he'd left her. She'd moved on. But he still wanted to make her smile and protect her from the world. Too bad the greatest danger she'd faced before all this had been from him.

Well, not anymore. Now at least he would protect her from Hugh and his men. Then he'd leave. He'd become part of his daughter's life, but that was it. And it was best this way.

Faded sunlight reflected off the snow, and the day of his accident replayed through his mind in vivid pictures. The high-energy ski event, a double black diamond course, the arrogant skier who challenged him to race a course he'd never run before, a quick glance that hadn't been long enough to show him the evergreen that hovered along the slope like a giant knife.

He'd been a cocky young man, desperate to prove himself. But maybe that was the problem—maybe, like Everly said, he *didn't* need to prove himself. To her especially.

Isaac jogged through the community gates, to

the wide fields abutting the road. He set his feet in the boots, pulled the goggles over his face and shoved off. The whooshing wind whistled past. The first stretch was straight, easy. The mechanics of cross-country skiing returned, and his muscles flowed into the motions as he followed the road they'd driven here on. How long would it take to get back to Eichhorns?

A flash of black and silver caught his eye from the slope to his left. A snowmobile?

Pop-pop-pop noises whizzed around him, striking a nearby tree and dinging one of his poles. One of Hugh's men was firing at him.

He ducked low and shoved the poles in the ground, zigzagging across the open field. The wind screamed in his ears, and pain burned his arm from the barbed-wire wound.

His speed increased, but it was still no match for the powerful snowmobile roaring toward him. Was it one of the new ones Everly mentioned earlier?

Isaac bent forward, digging hard with the poles, angling toward a thick wall of trees on the opposite side of the field. He'd have to go for cover if he hoped to survive this encounter.

More shots fired, pinging into the tree trunks yards away. His lungs churned through the oxygen and his muscles burned with exertion. There! He flew through the tree line, barely avoiding a collision with a prickly evergreen trunk. Snow plonked down on him from the branches. The copse of trees appeared about fifty yards deep. Not enough coverage.

No other choice.

Isaac slackened his pace, maneuvering through the foliage as sweat trickled down his back, beneath his coat. His throat was so dry his tongue stuck to the roof of his mouth.

The buzzing of the snowmobile drew closer. The man was following Isaac into the trees.

Isaac shoved the poles into the packed snow and unlatched his boots. He stooped behind a huge stump, gripping a ski across his lap. The black machine ate up the ground, spitting out snow and crunching through the woods.

Isaac's jaw unhinged. No way could that machine make it without an impact of some sort.

"Over here!" He jumped up, waving, then sank back behind the cover.

Fifteen yards away. Ten. Headed right for him. Five. The dark, narrowed eyes of the man recklessly driving the machine met Isaac's.

Two. *Now!*

Isaac leaped to his feet, swinging the ski like an oddly-shaped baseball bat at the man's shoulders and head. The man flung the closest arm out to deflect the blow and shouted in pain as his arm smashed back into his chest. A crack echoed off the trunks.

The driver tumbled off the snowmobile, landing in a heap as the machine coasted forward a couple of feet before coming to a standstill.

The perp curled in a ball on his side, groaning.

Isaac was on him, snatching the gun from the man's waistband, then landing a jab to his head when he tried to move. It was James.

"You again?"

A moan rose from the injured man's mouth. Superficial wounds marked his cheeks and scalp from the fall and the sharp branches, plus the wounded arm held across his middle. Nothing fatal. Isaac shoved the gun into James's shoulder, searching for the man's cell phone. There. He tugged it out. "Where's Everly?"

"I don't know."

Isaac put pressure on the man's arm, eliciting a howl of pain. "I think you do."

"She's in a cabin."

"There are a dozen cabins on this side of the resort. Which one?"

"Patrol."

The ski patrol cabin. "What's the code into your phone?"

"What? You can't use—"

Isaac settled more of his weight on James's

injury. The man ground out an oath, then murmured a number Isaac didn't quite catch. "What's that?"

James growled out the number again, then moaned, his eyes rolling back in his head and his body going slack.

Isaac leapt onto the snowmobile. His muscles tightened as he settled on the machine and familiarized himself with the controls. A quick glance back confirmed the man still lay on the ground at an awkward angle. Passed out. Isaac shoved the gun into his waistband and tapped the cell phone's code. It worked. He added Dan's number and sent a quick text, then revved the engine and took off.

FIFTEEN

The rope around Everly's wrists chafed her skin, and her eyes struggled to adjust to the dark room. Where had James taken her?

She'd woken up moments ago to find her arms behind her, tied tightly to a heavy wooden chair set in the center of a large room. From the way shadows played over the wall and floor, it appeared to be a supply room of some sort. A table lined with boxes sat along the far wall, and more chairs were stacked in the corner. Next to them was a small fridge with a first aid kit on top, and some discarded snowshoes lay on the floor. Why would a—wait. She was in the ski patrol cabin, which was situated only a few hundred yards from Hugh's condo.

She wiggled her arms, squirmed her legs. The chair rocked slightly, but the ropes held. She was trapped. Would anyone even know to look for her here?

Isaac. Had he gotten out of the townhouse, or had that blast—

"He's alive." Speaking it aloud kept the fear of it from burrowing beneath her skin and even deeper. She shook her head. He couldn't be gone. He'd just returned and… Everly closed her eyes and was instantly transported back to that horrible avalanche, stuck beneath all that snow. Completely alone.

Except she wasn't.

God had been with her, just as He was now. He'd protected her. Guided her through the storms she'd faced so far. Isaac's reminder from the pit echoed in her heart. *For we walk by faith, not by sight.* She was blind in this situation, but she would trust God to lead her.

She positioned her hands lower and rubbed the rope against the back edge of the chair. The friction twisted her wrists tighter, burning the sensitive skin but loosening the tension in the rope. After a minute she stopped, alarmed at how hot the area felt on her skin.

A man's voice startled her, carrying in from the front room. She couldn't make out words, but she'd know the speaker even with a blindfold on.

The door flung open, and daylight blinded her. She tucked her chin and shut her eyes as footsteps closed in. Everly blinked, squinting up into a familiar face.

Hugh.

"Why did you kill Lars?" she demanded.

"Me?" He drew back, his air of surprise at odds with the gleam in his beady eyes. "I don't know what you're talking about. The police found a bloody shirt in *your* office. I should be asking you the same question."

"You know very well I didn't kill him. What I want to know is *why* you're doing this."

"No, I'm giving orders here, not you. Here's what's going to happen. You're going to sign this confession letter—" he waved a piece of paper in the air "—and admit you killed Lars and set fire to the chalet to cover it up. You'll also admit you ended Mr. Rhodes's life because of what he did to you. Leaving you alone, pregnant years ago."

Her heart pumped out a denial. What happened to her after she signed it? Hannah's sweet little smile tugged at the frayed pieces of her heart. "No one who knows me will believe it."

"They'll have no choice. You'll be dead, and the last piece of you will be this letter admitting all you've done."

"You make me sick."

"Unfortunately, not. I realized too late I've been poisoning the wrong Raven." Hugh bent closer, the sneer on his face within striking distance. She twisted her wrists in desperation, but the rope wouldn't budge. Instead, she shrank back as Hugh's rank breath wafted into her face. "Your father was easy enough of an obstacle to move out of my way. You, not so much."

"Move out of your way? Why?"

"Come on, are you that clueless?"

He wanted full ownership. "Wasn't running this place enough?"

"No. Ravens needs a new owner. A new name. A new start to be the best ski resort in New England."

"What about Lars?" She nipped at her lower lip to hide its trembling. At the least, she needed to buy herself as much time as possible by tossing questions at him.

"Ah, good old Lars. A lifelong friend, that one."

"How can you call yourself his friend? You're a backstabber. You murdered him!"

"Let's just say that three is an awkward number. Me, your father *and* Lars. You see, Lars was supposed to help me secure that bid for the US Alpine Challenge, not refuse to sign off on the paperwork. He is the backstabber. He owed it to me."

"What do you mean, *he owed it to you*? Because you two worked together in Park City?"

"Someone's been snooping in on my life." Hugh clicked his tongue. "Our ski business would've taken off except for Lars's foolishness. *He* made the mistake of selling damaged ski gear, which led to a customer's serious injury and a lawsuit, which became the downfall of our successful business. I could've ruined him if I shared what he'd done."

That sounded like an unfortunate mistake to her. "So, you forced him to *recommend* you to my dad and help get you hired here."

"That's correct." He nodded as if they were having a regular conversation and not discussing a dead man's mistakes. "I had big plans for this place. All of these upgrades had to be done in order to host the Alpine Challenge and then, the World Skiing Championships after that. But all that changed when Lars suddenly decided he wanted no part of my plans." He sighed theatrically, but a dark undertone tainted his words. "Lars was always weak. A distraction from the goal. And he especially didn't care for your father's involvement with his wife."

The fight seeped from her muscles. Her dad…and *Ingrid*?

"Ah, you didn't know." Hugh drew closer and lifted her chin with one finger, holding it in place by pressing on her jaw. Everly cringed at his overpowering cologne and sweaty skin and the way he stared at her like she was a bug under his microscope.

"You're disappointed in your father's behavior. I'm not. At least he fell for it so I didn't have to kill him too. Ingrid was a beautiful distraction. She loves the attention, you know, always has some fella she's pulling along on a leash."

She yanked away from his painful grasp. Poor Lars. What had he hidden beneath his steady, quiet exterior all these years? And her dad. Was that why Ingrid had visited him in the hospital? Disappointment dogged each inhale and exhale of her aching lungs.

She needed to keep asking questions. *Keep him distracted.* "How did you plant that shirt in my office?"

"I have my ways, Ms. Raven. People listen to you, and I have people who listen to me."

"Not many."

His lip curled. "You just be glad that shirt caught the police officer's attention. The next step in the plan had to do with your sweet little daughter."

Anger burst behind her eyes. She shoved her feet under the chair, lifting it so it jumped forward and she knocked into Hugh, sending him to his backside.

He swore, regained his balance, then whipped around behind her, hands clamping her shoulders like a metal bear trap. She groaned as he squeezed harder and harder.

"Your father was right about you. You are tough. Maybe you could have run this place, but you would've kept it the same. Boring. Same old slopes, no challenge to the best skiers. No growth. No new, bigger competitions."

"It's too late, Hugh. Just turn yourself in. There's a man in Park City who—ow!" Her eyes watered as his grip intensified.

"His testimony means nothing. Raven's will be so much more under *my* leadership. Imagine the crowds, the name recognition. The revenue. We'll bring in the best skiers, best snowboarders. Host the biggest competitions, right here in Maple Creek. Bring this boring little town to life finally. Right now, Raven's is a Podunk family joint where the slopes are covered with little kids who can't stand up and old people who think they can ski."

"That's the heart of Raven's, Hugh. You can't change that."

"I already am. With your father's health failing and his devastation from your death, he'll be eager to sell the resort to me for cheap." He left the room, then strode back in with a green coffee mug that said Raven's Fun Runs in wide black lettering. Dark liquid sloshed over the edges.

"I hope you like your coffee black and deadly."

Adrenaline emptied into her numb limbs, tingling her skin. Was he going to poison her? "I won't drink it."

"Yes, you will. If you sign the paper and drink this willingly now, your daughter will remain safe. Your fate will match that of Lars's. We'll turn it into a lovers' quarrel, with a messy murder-suicide. I can even tie in your father's illness by saying it was you."

"My family knows I would never do that. I love my dad!" Despite his interference with Isaac and his weakness with Ingrid, he was still her only living parent. "And Lars was my mentor. That was it. Everyone here knows that."

"Do they? Your father isn't himself these days. He's been ill and unreliable. And from what I've heard about Isaac, he didn't even care that he left a child behind."

"You have no idea what you're talking about." Everly sank her chin to her chest as fear for her daughter consumed her.

The need to keep him talking, to stay alive longer, pressed her pulse into overdrive. "Who else are you working with? James, Abbot and Eddy? Is that it? Detective Savage? Who did you send after us at the hospital?"

"Enough questions! I know what you're doing. You're stalling me. But the real question is—what are you going to do? Sign the paper, drink this, and your daughter stays safe. Might even still grow up on this resort under Uncle Hugh's guidance and protection. Refuse to drink it, and you still die. My men will toss your body along with your daughter's where they'll never be found. No one will know what happened."

Fury tinged her vision red and black. She spat on him. "You're disgusting."

Hugh wiped at the spittle on his pants, his features contorting with rage. "Enough! You have thirty seconds to decide."

Everly saw her chance. Her hands might be tied but her lower body wasn't.

She bent over, real tears turning into her last hope, soaking her cheeks. "I d-don't know what t-to d-do…" Her sobs were loud and high-pitched, not the way she usually cried.

"Shut up! I don't have time for this."

She continued wailing, her neck and face curled forward, whole body shaking. *Please, God.*

He stepped so close his shoes nearly touched hers. "Stop your blubbering or I'll—"

Everly drew her right leg up hard and fast into the wrist holding the mug. He grunted and turned away, half of the hot liquid splashing onto his shirt. His furious cry shook her eardrums. He muttered an oath and flung the mug at her. The edge grazed her cheek, then smashed into her shoulder before crashing to the floor. The ceramic mug exploded, and pain seared the side of her head, making her dizzy. Everly threw her other knee up, pushing her foot into Hugh's soft belly. He growled and flailed backward, arms pedaling the air.

Hugh hit the tile floor with a howl of pain.

The momentum caused the chair to fall forward, and Everly landed on his legs, then slammed sideways on her arm. Pain burst from the spot, and her cry joined Hugh's. She scooted the chair in an awkward side crawl, smashing it into a wall. The frame of it crumpled, loosening her wrists.

Hugh struggled to his feet. "Oh no, you don't!"

Everly disentangled her arms, then levered the broken chair at him, sending it across the floor, but he kicked it away with a furious swipe.

She rose, facing him on trembling legs, her heart thrashing in her chest.

"Looks like—" He grabbed for her.

She ducked, darting sideways, but his hands were everywhere. Squeezing. Scratching.

"—you'll die here." Hugh shoved her, sending her reeling into the wall. The impact knocked the remaining breath out of her. "And so will your daughter."

A shadow appeared behind Hugh. James was back? *Please, God, not like this.*

The shadow slipped into the room and swung a long wooden object at Hugh, connecting in a crack of bone and force that sent the resort manager flying sideways.

"You are not touching my daughter!"

Hugh collapsed to the floor in a broken heap.

She gaped across the room, relieved tears blurring her vision. "Isaac?"

"Everly." Isaac wielded a child's wooden sled. "You're alive."

She untangled her quivering legs and tried to stand. Isaac flung the sled down and rushed over, drawing her into his steady embrace. His gentle palms framed her face as he scrutinized every inch. "Did you drink any of it?"

"No, no. I knocked it over and it s-spilled."

Isaac's hands swept up her arms, then he flicked out his pocketknife and cut the rest of the rope from her wrists. "You're bleeding."

"It was the m-mug. I'm okay. You're here." He was still alive! She wouldn't believe it except she could feel his arms around her. "What happened at Hugh's? They threw the bomb inside and then everything went dark. The other guy was going around—"

"He's dead. It was Abbot. The bomb blasted a hole between the first and second floors. Then I found skis, and James came after me when I was skiing back to Fall Line Road. He told me where you were. He's in custody now." He stepped away and surveyed the room before returning his attention to her. "I'm sorry I didn't get here in time to stop this." He stroked the wound on her neck.

"It's okay. I'm just glad you're safe and we're…" *Together.* She paused, suddenly unsure of herself. Unsure of what to say to him. Was the danger truly past? Her tense muscles loosened until she wasn't sure she could continue standing.

He wrapped an arm around her as though he'd read her mind, and she sagged into him. "Hugh's done."

A sob worked its way up her throat. "I can't believe it's f-finally over."

"Hugh was no match for Everly Raven."

"Yeah, my distracting him worked for a while, but *you* got Hugh on the ground. *You* saved me. Again."

"Guess we're good at watching out for each other." He leaned forward and set his forehead to hers. Everly closed her eyes as her heart beat out wave after wave of relief and gratitude.

"I need to update Dan." He pulled away, withdrawing a cell phone from his pocket.

He was all business again.

"That's not your phone."

"No, my phone disappeared after the bomb at Hugh's place. This is James's phone. I, uh, got the code out of him, and I've been communicating with Dan this way."

She frowned at Hugh, crumpled on the chalet floor. "What do we do with him?"

"Hugh gets a pair of shiny bracelets to wear." Isaac tucked the cell away, then dangled another pair of handcuffs he must have picked up on their helicopter ride yesterday. "Let's get him to the authorities, you can explain all this to your dad, then we'll—"

She waited, but he didn't finish the statement. Instead, his eyes roved over the room again. Was he avoiding looking at her?

"The lab report for Park City was already emailed to the sheriff's office and to our headquarters. The witness in Park City said he has emails from Hugh about the money trafficking scheme when they served on the USSA board together. An arrest warrant is out for Hugh now. The local PD are searching Hugh's place now too. Though there's not much left to see after the explosion.

"Dan sent a chopper. It should be here any

minute." He clasped her hand, threading their fingers, then securing them inside his other hand like he held a precious jewel in his grasp. "Think you can stand riding in one again?"

Her heart walloped against her ribs, but it wasn't from having to ride in a helicopter. "I can handle it."

Isaac settled into the chopper's narrow seat beside Everly. She continued trembling, even when he placed the emergency blanket over her torso and shoulders. He wasn't sure whether it was from being cold, from the traumatizing events she'd just been through or from riding in a helicopter again. Likely all of it. After all, Everly had nearly taken out Hugh on her own, with her hands tied, too.

She was one tough woman, and he couldn't be prouder of her. He shook off the rush of feelings and mentally filed through the events of the last hour. The local PD pilot had hovered in the nearby field as Isaac helped Everly inside, then shoved a moaning, handcuffed Hugh onto the dirty floor.

Where he belonged.

When the helicopter landed at the pad in the valley minutes later, Dan's rental Suburban and an unmarked Maple Creek police cruiser met them. Everly clambered down onto the footplate, then Isaac dragged Hugh out. They headed toward the vehicles, Isaac lugging the semiconscious Hugh, and Everly limping slightly ahead. A muscular, brown-haired man exited the cruiser and stood beside Dan, his stance and expression grave. Who was that?

Everly paused mid-stride. "Detective Savage."

Isaac shouldered Hugh's bulk through the snow surrounding the landing pad, trailing off to the parked vehicles. He wrangled Hugh inside the police cruiser, then shut the door. Once he sidled up to Everly again he addressed Dan. "Brought you something." He nodded at the stranger. "Detective. I'm Isaac Rhodes."

"Agent Rhodes." Savage's shrewd gaze swept over him before jumping to Hugh, crumpled inside his vehicle. "Well done." He spoke to Everly. "Seems you were caught up in a sabotage plan, Ms. Raven."

She rubbed her palms lightly over her poor, scratched face. "No kidding. I just wish you'd figured that out right away."

Savage let out an abbreviated chuckle. "Yes, well, Hugh Markham did his legwork before murdering Lars Henken. Someone on his team phoned in a tip after the murder, said you and Lars Henken had an argument not long ago, maybe two weeks? Suggested—well, regardless, when I contacted a couple resort patrons who'd been staying here at the time of your argument, they confirmed hearing it."

Guilt and regret chased across her face. "We had a minor disagreement in the lobby of the main lodge about some resort business. I didn't realize patrons overheard it."

Anger simmered in Isaac's gut as he spoke to Detective Savage. "That's why you were on her trail after the chalet blew?"

Savage nodded. "Correct. With Hugh riding my tail as much as I was riding hers."

"Lars was my friend. I couldn't..." Everly's tone wavered, her words humming with emotion. "I would never have hurt him."

When she sniffled, Isaac ignored protocol, wrapping his arm around her again. A good friend, offering support. That was it. She drooped against him, wiping her eyes. "I'm so glad this is all over."

"Me too," Isaac whispered. But didn't that mean he'd never be able to do what he was doing right now—holding her, supporting her? Despair speared his chest.

She pressed her face to his shoulder. "I just want to get Hannah and go somewhere safe and warm and sleep for a week."

A car door slammed behind them, and they turned to find a tall, slender woman in dark slacks exiting an expensive sport utility vehicle. The upper portion of her face was covered by large, dark sunglasses, and her spiked blond hair struck a memory chord.

"Is that—"

"Ingrid."

Ingrid rushed over, arms out. "Ev, what happened? Are you okay, sweetie?" She extricated a limp Everly from Isaac's arms and pointed at her SUV. "Why don't I take her home?"

Savage held up a finger. "She needs to get to the station first to give her statement." He aimed the finger at Isaac. "You both do. How about you take her there, Mrs. Henken, and we'll ride over after you. I have a couple more points to cover with the agents."

Isaac tried to catch Everly's eye, but she was already turned away, guided by Ingrid's firm hands. "I'll catch up to you in a few minutes, okay?" he called out.

Everly finally swiveled around, a weary expression tugging at her lips. "Okay. See you soon."

He watched as the two women loaded into the SUV and drove off. How he longed to wrap up this investigation and carve out some time to talk to Everly, just the two of them. His heart churned wildly. And Hannah.

Savage's cell chimed. "Hold up, gentlemen."

He withdrew it and set it against his ear. "Savage here." A long pause, and his dark eyes blinked in confusion then narrowed. "Okay. I'll pass that information on." He pressed the end call button. "We have a problem."

Isaac's spine snapped straight. "What is it?"

Savage crossed his arms over his barrel chest. "The bloody shirt we found in Ms. Raven's office was sent to the lab. I asked them to rush it."

"It's not Everly Raven's shirt?" Dan interrupted.

"No, it is Ms. Raven's shirt." The detective cocked his head. "That part was true. And the blood appears to be Lars's. The problem is Ms. Raven submitted a DNA sample when I first interviewed her, and though the hairs *are* from a female, they don't match hers."

Isaac jerked his head back. "Who would they belong to then?"

"Ingrid Henken."

Isaac sucked in a hasty breath. Ingrid. She must've been part of Hugh's sabotage plan too, and Everly was with her right now. He shoved his hand toward Dan. "I need your keys!"

Dan tossed the set across the snowy ground. He snatched them midair and sprinted to the SUV.

Everly leaned back against the headrest. Ingrid's car smelled like money and leather and

whatever perfume she doused herself with, and
it turned Everly's stomach. She ignored the nausea and pictured Hannah's sweet face.

All she could think about was giving her
statement and getting back to Hannah. Wrapping her daughter in a long hug and introduc-
ing Isaac to her.

"What a mess this situation has turned into,"
Ingrid railed. "I mean, first Lars and now the
feds get involved. I can't believe Hugh did this.
It's just…too much." She pounded a fist to the
steering wheel.

"I am so sorry about Lars. At least it's all
over. Finally."

"Right. *All over*," Ingrid muttered, her features twisted in irritation.

Everly glanced her way, but the other woman
averted her face to concentrate on Fall Line
Road.

Was Ingrid aware of all that Hugh had done?
Did she know he'd murdered Lars? From the
sound of it, she'd been too busy pursuing Everly's dad the past few months to care. The nausea in her stomach hardened into resentment. If
Everly had been paying better attention, maybe
she could've put a stop to the older woman's
interest in her dad. Everly shifted her head,
eyeing Ingrid's perfectly styled hair and designer clothes.

It hurt to know Ingrid had betrayed Lars with her dad, and that Dad had fallen for it.

Everly released a slow sigh. "I just want to hold my little girl again."

"And that handsome hunk of FBI agent, too, I imagine?" Ingrid giggled, the sound at odds with her previous angry tone.

Everly pictured Isaac. His smile, the way his strong arms fit perfectly around her when she needed them. The way he'd rescued her an hour ago and two days before that. "No, we're not…" Her heart dipped and soared, betraying her words. "I'm just grateful he came back."

"Yes, how convenient for you."

A strange undercurrent of frustration wrapped the woman's statement. Maybe her dad's opinion of Isaac had rubbed off on Ingrid. "Are you upset he came back? I didn't think you cared about him, back when we married."

Ingrid flicked her fingers. "It doesn't matter now. Let's get you to your daughter and then we'll worry about the rest."

Everly sat up, and the seat belt tightened across her chest like a fabric arm. They were near the entrance to Raven's, the welcoming wrought iron gates strung with little white lights not far off in the distance. "I thought we were going to the police station first?"

"Plans changed a bit, sweetie."

Ingrid's flippant tone sent a cold prickle of alarm across Everly's skin. "I think we should do what the detective said."

"That detective has no idea what he's talking about. And right now, I'm in charge. First, we're getting your daughter, then I'll figure out what happens next."

"No." Alarm transformed into terror, and certainty cemented inside her that she did not want Hannah inside this vehicle with this woman. "I don't want to get my daughter yet."

Ingrid jammed on the brakes, and the vehicle's back tires spun out from under them. Everly screamed as they slid across the road, then slammed to a stop.

"Why—what are you doing, Ingrid?"

"Cleaning up the mess."

"You're not making any sense. What mess? Hugh's already arrested." Everly inched back toward the passenger window, one hand searching for her seat-belt clasp. Had Ingrid not only gone after her dad, but also been in on the sabotage plan with Hugh?

"Don't bother. My car is locked. You're not going anywhere."

Everly's tongue went cotton-ball dry, and fear tingled through her fingers and toes. "Please, Ingrid. Take me to the police station."

"No," she snapped, then inhaled sharply as

though trying to calm herself. "We're not going there today."

The urge to unravel this sudden, unexpected mystery and keep Ingrid distracted pried Everly's tongue loose from her bone-dry mouth. "Where *are* we going, then?"

"Stop asking questions!" Ingrid screeched, accelerating so the vehicle rocked forward. She hit the brakes again, and they careened into a snowbank. "Now look what you made me do!" She threw it in Reverse and revved the engine. The tires spun loudly on the snow, then they caught, shooting the SUV backward onto the road.

Everly clenched her jaw at the jerky movements. "You're working with Hugh, aren't you? You weren't even interested in my dad. Only his money."

"I don't want his *money*. I wanted this resort. This land. All of it. And I deserve it. I should be the head ski instructor, not my spineless husband." She threw her hands out, a nail nicking Everly's cheek while the others clacked into the driver's window. "Your father was incredibly gullible, but that's a man for you."

"How about trusting? My dad and I trusted you people! And Lars? You knew about Hugh killing him?" Her head pounded as she shouted back at Ingrid.

"Knew? Sweetheart, I did it myself."

Everly's mouth fell open.

"How do you think he got up to Tipping Point? I led him there. Begged him to forgive me for romancing your dad. I even promised to work on our *failing marriage*." She used air quotes and rolled her eyes. "Way back when we were in youth skiing, Lars had this do-gooder streak. It was cute, really. But unfortunately, it got in the way of our plans. All of my plans. When he admitted what he'd done at the ski store, we lost the business. Did Hugh mention that, hmm? A lady ended up paralyzed because of the broken skis Lars sold her."

"That was a terrible accident." Everly's rib cage expanded then contracted with sorrow and shock. What a burden Lars must've carried from that incident, and then Hugh—and Ingrid—held it over his head. How awful.

There had to be a way out of this situation. An opportunity to incapacitate Ingrid. *Please, God, show me what to do.* Everly turned slightly, scoping around the vehicle. A department store bag lay on the back seat, crumpled. Nothing else behind her. She wriggled her shoes. Something long and thin but heavy sat near her feet. An ice scraper?

"Don't even think about it, Ms. Raven." Ingrid cocked her head, the attractive symmetry of her features marred by the hatred on her face.

"You and Hugh deserve each other. And neither of you deserve this resort."

"I deserve Raven's much more than you, you spoiled child. You've had your chance to make this place bigger and better, to host major skiing events and put us on the map, and you failed. Your time here is over."

Disbelief tunneled Everly's vision. "Do you actually still think there's a chance you could run the resort?" Didn't Ingrid realize the police and the feds had Hugh, and they'd be on to her?

"You will never understand what it's like to be so close to winning, so close to having something you've wanted your whole life, only to have it yanked away. Again, and again."

Isaac's face spread through her mind. Maybe Everly did know what that was like.

"It doesn't matter." Ingrid's nails left indentations on the steering wheel. "The bottom line is you're in the way. You and your daughter. And I'm tired of it." Ingrid leaned across the middle console and opened the glove compartment. Everly recoiled at the small black gun nestled inside. "At least I secured Lars's life insurance policy. The money will keep me going after I leave this boring little town." Ingrid angled her head so they made eye contact, a broken smile covering her bloodred lips. "And some satisfaction after you bungled up our plan."

Everly's gaze flew from Ingrid's face to the gun and back. Then she reacted. She brought her elbow down on the arm Ingrid used to reach for the weapon. Ingrid let out a startled cry, and Everly shoved the heel of her palm to her seatbelt lock. It clicked but didn't release. She tried again, fumbling to unlock the door at the same time. But Ingrid reached to her left and jabbed the lock button, snarling out an oath.

A huge black shadow approached the driver's side of the vehicle as Ingrid cocked her arm, gun in hand, to shoot Everly at close range. "You're not going—"

Ingrid's scream shattered the air just as the glass splintered inches behind her. Dan's SUV! It crashed into the left side of the car, crunching up the door and pushing Ingrid's car sideways, pinning Ingrid in her seat belt. The gun clattered to the floor.

A man jumped out of the dark vehicle that hit them and circled Ingrid's. *Isaac!* Everly punched the seat belt again and manually unlocked her door, slamming herself sideways as the door gave. She tumbled to the snow, flailing for something steady to anchor herself to.

Isaac caught her, lifting her against his chest. "Everly! Are you okay? Did she—"

"Isaac!" She burrowed into him, gripping his jacket and broad shoulders. "She didn't get a chance to sh-shoot me. You stopped her in time."

"It's okay. I'm here. I'm here." He crushed her gently to him. "I'm not going anywhere again."

His determined words broke through her pain and shock. Did he mean—?

"Stay here for a moment." He pointed to a nearby stump. "I need to make sure Ingrid is subdued."

She nodded and sank onto the wood. He let go and rose, then disappeared into Ingrid's vehicle. The metallic crank of handcuffs along with Ingrid's wounded moan drew another sob from her chest. Was this truly it? Were she and Hannah and Isaac finally safe?

Isaac leaped out and crouched in front of her. "She's handcuffed. I'm here. You're safe," he murmured as though he'd read her mind.

His strong hands cupped her cheeks, lifting her hair to inspect her neck and face. Then he swept her close again, and Everly reveled in the steady beat of his heart near her ear.

He spoke into her hair. "I'm sorry I let you leave with her. Right after she drove off, Savage got a call that it was her DNA on the bloody shirt. Then when I caught up to you, I saw you two tussling in there and I just—"

"Crashed into us." An onslaught of tears blurred her vision, but she let them fall because they were from relief and gratitude. "I'm so glad it was you. Only you." Did he understand what she meant? So much more than the words she'd spoken.

"Only me?" He pulled back so he could gaze in her eyes. "Everly?"

She smiled at him through the tears trickling down her cheeks, then gave a nod.

He gently rubbed them away with the pad of his thumb. "When we got married, our vows spoke of commitment and love. I bombed on the first one, but I excelled at the second. I've never stopped loving you. Do you see that? You were always with me, Everly."

"You still love me?"

"Yes, I still love you. I kept those snowshoes because they were proof that you'd once loved me, too. May I...?"

She nodded again, and he drew her close. Their lips met, the old and the new sealing together in a tender promise of the future.

She cupped his cheek. "I love you, too, Isaac. Still. Always. When I saw you in the cabin the other day, it felt like a missing piece of myself came back. I just...didn't recognize it right away. And I'm sorry I let my dad scare you away after your accident."

"I shouldn't have listened to him, and to my doubts. I can't stand the thought of being away from you and Hannah for another day."

She pressed another kiss to his lips. "You don't have to." Their future surrounded them, pure white with forgiveness and stretching into forever.

EPILOGUE

"Ready to meet your daughter?" Everly cut the Jeep's ignition and smiled at him.

"I've been ready ever since you told me about her."

With Everly safe, Ted Raven notified about the shocking events at Raven's and Dan taking over the brunt of the case for now, Isaac should've slept well last night. Instead, he'd tossed and turned in the spare bed above Eichhorns, picturing Hannah. Longing to meet her.

Everly had spent a couple of hours in the ER, getting her wounds treated before returning to her apartment to reunite with their daughter and her friend.

Today was the day for introductions. For new beginnings.

"What if she doesn't like me?" He dashed a hand through his hair. Sheila had trimmed it last night, and the shorter length felt strange.

Everly stroked his shoulder. "She'll love you too. Just give her time to warm up."

He closed the gap and pressed a soft kiss to her mouth, entwining their fingers. This he would never take for granted again. "I'm never letting go."

"Me either."

Eichhorns—and the entire resort—bustled with life today. Maple Creek residents and Raven's employees filled the dining room, conversations lowering when he and Everly entered, hands clasped.

Sheila's friendly smile welcomed them in. "'Bout time you two lovebirds showed up."

Isaac took it all in, his heart pumping twice as fast as it needed to. In a corner booth, Becca waited alongside a bouncy, dark-haired little girl.

Hannah.

Everly led him through the tables, greeting a few people on the way. The eager ache building in his chest grew to painful proportions as they approached.

"Mommy!" Hannah leaped from the seat straight into Everly's arms, her little body locking with her mom's. "Where'd you go?"

Isaac gulped at the sight of Everly—his wife—holding their daughter. He stood off to the side, an observer longing to be a participant.

"I was checking on Alpine. And I brought a friend for you to meet. This is Mr. Isaac."

When Everly motioned at him, his pulse double-timed. He gave Becca a nod but couldn't take his eyes off Hannah. Her heart-shaped face and soft brown curious eyes. Part him and part Everly. His throat thickened, and he clenched his hands to keep from reaching out to make sure she was real. His daughter wouldn't be ready for a hug just yet.

"Hi, Mr. Isaac." A quick flash of teeth, then she ducked into her mom's shoulder.

"Hannah, I'm really glad I get to meet you."

"Why?"

Her naive directness brought a grin to his mouth. "Well, your mom told me stories about you. You sound so fun, I wanted to meet you."

Her lips pouted when she took her mom's measure, then looked back at him. "Did she say I'm a big girl?"

"She did say that. She also said you like to color." He pulled a pack of crayons from his jacket pocket along with two sheets of folded paper. "Would you like to…draw me a picture?"

Hannah's delighted squeal reached the rafters. "Mommy, he has a pwesent for me!" Hannah bounced in Everly's arms. "Canna have it?"

"What do you say when someone gives you a gift?" She gazed over their daughter's head at him, and he prayed the gratitude in his heart was obvious in his eyes.

She'd given *him* the gift. *A second chance. Their daughter.*

"Thank you," he murmured at the same time Hannah sang *Fank you, fank you.*

He handed her the box of crayons, their fingers brushing. Everly set Hannah down beside Becca, then she and Isaac folded to sit at the booth on the opposite side.

He couldn't take his eyes off their daughter as she went to work on a picture. A shadow fell over the table just then, and Isaac looked up. Ted Raven.

He started to stand, but Ted pressed a hand on his shoulder. "No need to get up."

"Poppy!" Hannah bobbed in her seat.

"Hi, Dad," Everly said. "How are you feeling?"

"Hi, peanut." Ted chucked his granddaughter's chin, then addressed Everly. "Today I feel like a snowmobile hit me, not a Mack truck." He chuckled. "So, I'd say that's progress." His hazel gaze pinned Isaac. "I realize now that in my desperation to protect my daughter, I didn't cut you enough slack. I want you to know—" he paused like his next words cost him a great deal "—you're always welcome at Raven's."

He nodded at the man who'd once scorned

him. "Thank you, sir. I appreciate that." A dam broke in Isaac's chest, spilling relief through his system. Ted moved away to speak with a patron at the next table.

"What are you drawing?" Everly inquired of Hannah. Her hand found his under the table, threading them together.

"A pishure of me and Ow-pine. And you, Mommy. And Becca and Poppy." Hannah chewed her lower lip and stared over the table at him, something bright and compelling sparking in her little eyes. "And him, too, Mama? Him too?"

"What do you think, Isaac? Do you want to be in our picture?" She turned to face him, and at close range, the soft green in his wife's eyes turned his insides to melted snow.

"It's what I want most in the whole world."

* * * * *

If you enjoyed this book,
pick up these other exciting stories
from Love Inspired Suspense.

Arctic Witness
by Heather Woodhaven

Mountain Fugitive
by Lynette Eason

Covert Amish Investigation
by Dana R. Lynn

High Stakes Escape
by Elizabeth Goddard

Kidnap Threat
by Anne Galbraith

Find more great reads at
www.LoveInspired.com

Dear Reader,

Thank you so much for reading *Snowstorm Sabotage*! The story grew out of two aspects of my life. First, my New England childhood instilled a love of winter…sledding, ice skating and snow forts. Second, we visited a family ski resort while on vacation recently, and a story seed was planted.

In *Snowstorm Sabotage*, Everly feels lost and alone in the middle of a literal blizzard while she also faces a metaphorical storm in her life. If you're wandering in a storm, too, know that God is with you. He will guide you safely through. Just as Isaac recognized, I hope you know you're valuable and loved by the God who created snowflakes and snowcapped mountains.

I'd love to connect with you on my Facebook author page (Kerry Johnson, Author), Twitter and Instagram (@candidkerry), or my website, kerryjohnsonbooks.com, where you can sign up to receive my quarterly newsletter.

Fondly,
Kerry Johnson